Donald MacKenzie and The Murder Room

〉〉〉 This title is part of The Murder Room, our series dedicated to making available out-of-print or hard-to-find titles by classic crime writers.

Crime fiction has always held up a mirror to society. The Victorians were fascinated by sensational murder and the emerging science of detection; now we are obsessed with the forensic detail of violent death. And no other genre has so captivated and enthralled readers.

Vast troves of classic crime writing have for a long time been unavailable to all but the most dedicated frequenters of second-hand bookshops. The advent of digital publishing means that we are now able to bring you the backlists of a huge range of titles by classic and contemporary crime writers, some of which have been out of print for decades.

From the genteel amateur private eyes of the Golden Age and the femmes fatales of pulp fiction, to the morally ambiguous hard-boiled detectives of mid twentieth-century America and their descendants who walk our twenty-first century streets, The Murder Room has it all. **〉〉〉**

The Murder Room
Where Criminal Minds Meet

themurderroom.com

Donald MacKenzie 1908–1994

Donald MacKenzie was born in Ontario, Canada, and educated in England, Canada and Switzerland. For twenty-five years MacKenzie lived by crime in many countries. 'I went to jail,' he wrote, 'if not with depressing regularity, too often for my liking.' His last sentences were five years in the United States and three years in England, running consecutively. He began writing and selling stories when in American jail. 'I try to do exactly as I like as often as possible and I don't think I'm either psychopathic, a wayward boy, a problem of our time, a charming rogue. Or ever was.'

He had a wife, Estrela, and a daughter, and they divided their time between England, Portugal, Spain and Austria.

Henry Chalice

Salute from a Dead Man
Death Is a Friend
Sleep Is for the Rich

John Raven

Zalenski's Percentage
Raven in Flight
Raven and the Kamikaze
Raven and the Ratcatcher
Raven After Dark
Raven Settles a Score
Raven and the Paperhangers
Raven's Revenge

Raven's Longest Night
Raven's Shadow
Nobody Here By That Name
A Savage State of Grace
By Any Illegal Means
The Eyes of the Goat
The Sixth Deadly Sin
Loose Cannon

Standalone novels

Nowhere to Go
The Juryman
The Scent of Danger
Dangerous Silence
Knife Edge
The Genial Stranger
Double Exposure
The Lonely Side of the River
Cool Sleeps Balaban
Dead Straight
Three Minus Two
Night Boat from Puerto Vedra
The Kyle Contract
Postscript to a Dead Letter
The Spreewald Collection
Deep, Dark and Dead
Last of the Boatriders

The Kyle Contract

Donald MacKenzie

An Orion book

Copyright © The Estate of Donald MacKenzie 1970

The right of Donald MacKenzie to be identified as the author of this
work has been asserted in accordance with the Copyright, Designs and
Patents Act 1988.

This edition published by
The Orion Publishing Group Ltd
Orion House
5 Upper St Martin's Lane
London WC2H 9EA

An Hachette UK company
A CIP catalogue record for this book is available from the British Library

ISBN 978 1 4719 0583 4

www.orionbooks.co.uk

For Harlan and Harriet Carey
a tale about their native state

Brady Jordan   May 1969

HE WAS OUTSTANDING in a city where handsome men are
commonplace. A badger streak of white divided cropped
black hair. He was wearing a hand-stitched gray flannel
suit as if he knew that thirty-six was a good age and that a
few pounds overweight made no difference. He waited in
the bar alcove, scanning the crowded restaurant below. A
sweep of plate glass offered a panoramic view of the distant
hills. Their spring green was already rusting under the California sun. The place was new, drawing its clientele from
the higher echelons of the moving picture industry.

A short-jacketed barman drifted toward him, reaching for
a cocktail shaker. Jordan made a sign of dissent. The couple who had followed him in seated themselves at the bar.
The slacks the woman was wearing were an obvious mistake.
A pair of harlequin sunglasses rested on top of her orange-
tinted hair. Her companion's shirt was extravagant in cut
and color. The way he ordered their drinks seemed designed
to compensate for their appearance.

Jordan walked down the steps to the restaurant. He
knew without turning his head that the couple at the bar
were watching him in the mirror. A headwaiter material-
ized.

"Do you have a reservation, sir?" Hands and smile
flashed, demonstrating regret. "I'm sorry, sir. If you'd
care to take a seat at the bar I'll have a table for you in a few
minutes."

Jordan shook his head. "I've eaten, thanks. I'm joining

1

someone for coffee. Don't worry — I can see her over there."

He threaded his way across the room to a window table. The woman sitting there alone was in her late twenties. She looked up at him, letting a strand of strawberry blond hair fall in front of her eyes. She pushed it away and smiled. The gesture was studied but made with grace. The movement wafted the sharp scent of Ma Griffe into his nostrils. Her sleeveless dress of blue linen heightened her suntan.

He pulled a chair under him and made his apologies. "I'm sorry about that, Jo. You got my message OK?"

The half bottle of champagne in the ice bucket was upturned. The last of it was in her glass, the rest in the edginess of her voice.

"For God's sake, Brady! I haven't been stood up since I was sixteen. It's a new experience. Give me a cigarette."

She wiped her mouth with a napkin streaked with lipstick. He guessed that she must have made up many times during the past hour. He thumbed a cigarette from the pack and flicked her lighter. It was gold with the initials J.K. worked on the case in brilliants. The only jewelry she wore was a wedding ring.

"Something came up," he said carefully.

She dribbled a stream of smoke in his direction. "I'm sure. Don't tell me — let me guess. It was your agent. They need a writer out at Fox."

He felt the hot flush of blood above his collar. She had a talent for finding the right spot for her needle. He leaned forward, lowering his voice.

"You'd better listen to this, Jo. And I warn you, you're not going to like it."

She used the same stylized gesture as before, letting her shoulder-length hair swing in front of her face. Her voice was indulgent now.

"Don't I always listen to you, darling?"

He tapped a butt from the pack, lit it, and inhaled deeply. "You listen when it suits you. This is different. It involves us. We've known one another ten weeks, right?"

She posed prettily, cupping her chin in her hand as if accepting a compliment. "Ten weeks and two days to be exact. And who says romance is dead! There was I in a headscarf — a Brentwood supermarket — and along comes this handsome stranger wheeling his little trolley full of groceries . . ."

He drove the answer at her, choosing it for shock value. "That was no chance meeting, Jo. I'd been following you for weeks looking for the chance to speak to you — the right moment. Your husband hired me to do it."

The clatter of table silver, the babble of the surrounding voices were loud as they looked at one another. Then she laughed.

"*Hired you? Sebastian!* I simply don't believe it."

He shrugged defensively. "You were never meant to, Jo. Can't you accept what I'm saying? This was a setup. Kyle's got a file on you that goes back six months."

"A file on *me*, sweetie?" Her voice was incredulous. "You have to be joking."

It was even tougher than he had expected and she was no help. "Steve Luckman," he said wearily. "That Dane out at Palm Springs — the tennis coach. Do I have to go on? Do you think I *like* remembering?"

3

Her slim fingers stretched out across the table, finding his. "You don't have to, darling. I swear it. That other stuff's history. I love you. *Tell* me . . ."

He tightened his grip on her hand. "I love you, Jo. That's why I'm here. I knew it right from the beginning. I went into this thing for money. Can't you realize how it's been for me over these last ten weeks? Knowing the way things were between us, not having the guts to tell you the truth. I was scared of losing you, Jo. Is that so wrong? But I can't go on like this any longer. Kyle's got to be told."

She released her fingers, worrying her lower lip with her teeth and staring through the window.

"I still can't believe it. Sebastian of all people. You mean he actually hired detectives? It's too ridiculous!"

He looked at her with compassion. She needed to be sure of herself more than anything in the world.

"Don't look now," he warned. "There's a couple sitting at the bar — a man and woman. They're from the Roscoe Agency in L.A. They specialize in divorce work and skip tracing. You've got to get this into your head, darling. Kyle's after your hide. You were too smart with the others. They could never get the evidence they needed for a divorce. I was supposed to be the guy who'd put that right. Kyle called the apartment early this morning. He left a message to call him back urgently. He was in conference; that's what kept me. He's sick of paying agency bills. He wants action."

She stubbed her cigarette out viciously. "Does he! And what did you charmers have in mind?"

He trapped her wrist again, forcing her to look at him.

"Not me, Jo, *him*. I want you to come away with me — not next week or next month but *now*."

Her glass was empty but she lifted it to her lips mechanically. "After Luckman and the Dane? There've been others, of course."

He closed his mind on the thought, wincing. "You love me," he said stubbornly.

She nodded vaguely. "I may love you, baby, but a girl gets a little shaken by a revelation of this kind. How much money has this English gentleman paid you?"

He found himself making the admission shamefully. "A few hundred dollars. Expenses. I was supposed to get five grand when the divorce came through."

She nibbled on a cuticle, her eyes on the couple at the bar. They were deep in conversation.

"Can you *prove* Sebastian gave you money?" she asked quietly.

He reached inside his jacket pocket. He had brought the two slips of paper to convince her. He passed them over the table. The first was an itemized phone bill from the Casablanca Apartments. The second was a check made out to Brady Jordan in the amount of three hundred and seventy-five dollars.

"It's the first check I ever had from him," he explained. "Normally he'd send cash in an envelope. Sometimes it would come from the Athletic Club or some hotel downtown. The agency doesn't know about this thing that Kyle and I have got going. They're playing me absolutely straight. It's a nice touch, isn't it? Take a look at that phone bill. Half those calls were made to your house."

Her fingers closed on the two pieces of paper. She stuffed them into her bag and wielded her lipstick with deft, sure strokes. He watched her, puzzled by the sudden switch in mood. She looked at him over the top of her hand mirror.

"I'm making no excuses, Brady. The truth's simple. I should never have married Sebastian in the first place. I've asked myself a thousand times since why I did it. Glamour, I guess. 'Fresno Divorcée Weds British Film Director.' And look what I got — a basic course on how to run a country house graciously. With an assist from that goddamn daughter of his and a housekeeper who fumigated the rooms after me. *Glamour!*" Her laugh was ugly. "I'm going to teach him a lesson, sweetheart. I'm going to take him for every penny he has and you're going to help me."

His green eyes clouded. "Not me, baby. I don't want any part of it."

She put her elbows on the table and her chin in her hand. She studied him for a while before answering.

"You want me, Brady, don't you? Or is that just another act?"

His face tightened. "You don't have the right to say that sort of thing and you know it. We don't need his money. We'll make out somehow."

She interlaced his fingers with hers. "*Somehow,* baby? The two of us living in a one-and-a-half room apartment — a charter-flight holiday to Hawaii once a year? You've been sitting around this town for over a year, over a year since you've even had an assignment. They're your words, Brady, not mine. Is that what you're offering me?"

The denial seemed pitifully thin. "We could move to Europe. I'd have a chance there. I could get work in Paris or Rome."

Her violet eyes had a sudden impatience. "For God's sake, come off it! This isn't a script, darling, it's life. *Our* life in a hard, hard town. What Sebastian's trying to do is criminal and that check proves it."

He almost gagged on the cold coffee. "Criminal?"

She sounded very sure of herself. "What else? He's trying to deceive the courts, isn't he?"

He blocked the next with upheld hand. "Are you saying that I'm part of a criminal conspiracy?"

She nodded. "Just that, darling. But don't worry, I'm not going to turn you in. I know my Sebastian. He might fool me once but it'll only *be* once. This evidence you were supposed to provide would never have been used. Not in a divorce court, anyway. No, he'd have blackmailed me with it. Blackmailed me to stay with him. I'd have eaten it with my meals. Slept with it from here to eternity."

He pushed his cup aside and called for the bill. The man and the woman were still at the bar, chatting animatedly. He knew the way they operated by now — knew most of them by sight. They'd split the moment he left Joanne. One would follow her, the other would tail him.

He signed the check, offering his credit card. There had been times when he'd been tempted to use this as a magic carpet. To take off on a spending spree and wind up on a beach in Brazil or somewhere with a trail of debts behind him that would set a record in the credit card business. Too many people had told him he was through in Hollywood. Too many of them were right. You could query the dramatic values of an assignment and get away with it. You could even imply that a director wasn't necessarily the best judge of how words should be put on paper. But the one thing no lousy writer with all his marbles *ever* did was join issue with a star. Especially when she had three and a half million dollars invested in her. Just once was enough. He could no longer drop in unannounced at his agent's and be sure of a welcome. Hell, he couldn't even get to Phil's secretary now, let alone Phil himself. After twelve years in the business he was walking the streets with a leper's bell tied around his neck. He looked across the table at her. "I'm listening," he said pointedly.

Her eyes were still hard. "We're setting up house, Brady baby. You and I. And Sebastian's paying for it. *I'm* the one who's suing for divorce, not him. He'll know that you'll testify against him. As long as I have this check, there's nothing he can do about it. You *would* testify, wouldn't you, Brady?"

He nodded, knowing that he was going her route, whatever it was.

"You'd better go home and pack your bags. I'll come with you."

She pinned her hair behind her ears with a black velvet band.

"Are you crazy? I'm not leaving the house till I've seen Liebowitz. He handled my last divorce. I can trust him. I want everything Sebastian has, not just half. Liebowitz knows the score. This is for us, darling. Believe me, I know what I'm doing."

He wasted time, putting his cigarettes in his pocket. "If Kyle gets his hands on that check and phone account you'll be wasting your time with a lawyer. Why don't you send them to Liebowitz?"

Her smile was faraway. "Because I don't trust *anyone* that much, baby. Liebowitz gets to see but not to keep. I'll leave the house when he says so. Meanwhile those papers stay right with Momma."

He had seen her in this kind of mood before but never so arrogant. "You're out of your mind," he objected. "*Where* for instance?"

The faraway look was secretive. "Right under my husband's nose. There's a loose board in a closet. I told you, I know what I'm doing, Brady, stop fussing. I've hidden things there before."

"Like letters from Luckman and the others." It was out before he could stop himself.

She reached across the table and put her fingertips on his mouth. "You're silly but I like it. I'll be at the beach house the same time as usual — OK?"

The busboy had cleared the table. The headwaiter was hovering expectantly.

"Tonight's supposed to be the night," Jordan said quietly. "You heard what I said. Kyle wants action. He knows we've been seeing one another at the beach house. I'm being tailed, for God's sake! They're going to be there with cameras tonight unless I call the whole thing off."

She sought her reflection in the mirror, the last reassurance before leaving, then his face. "Nobody'll be there. Sebastian wouldn't have the nerve after I get through with him. Don't you understand, I *want* him to know we're together tonight!"

He nodded resignedly and reached for her handbag. He covered the movement of his hand, dropping a twist of paper into the folds of her handkerchief.

"There's enough there for two joints. I'll bring more tonight. And don't get busted with it — it's good stuff."

She took the purse from him quickly. "Reliable Jordan."

He pushed his chair back. "Reliable Jordan. Let's get out of here. It's all right to take my arm. Those bums at the bar will expect it."

She rose, tanned, cool, and collected. "That's nice. We make a handsome couple. I hope they put it in their report."

There was a maliciousness in her voice that made him glad he wasn't in Kyle's shoes. The doorman brought her car. Jordan gave the man some change and handed her into the blue convertible. She was driving with the top down.

He craned over. "Don't do anything foolish now, hear?"

She drew on a pair of gloves, glancing away from the mirror. The woman from the bar had made her way outside. Her orange bangs appeared over the wheel of a black Ford parked up the street. Joanne's mouth thinned.

"I won't. Ten o'clock." She blew him a kiss and swung the convertible into the traffic. The black Ford pulled out after her.

Jordan watched the brake lights coming on and off till the two cars were well beyond the intersection. He walked around the block to the parking lot. The baldheaded man in the violent shirt was a cozy twenty yards behind. Jordan found his keys. He'd been telling the truth. Nobody at the Roscoe Agency knew of his contract with Kyle. He had played it straight for them from the beginning. He was still a little worried by Kyle's check. The Englishman had been so goddamn careful otherwise. He'd kept Jordan away from the house, had been adamant about the times when he would accept calls. This check was the first recorded link between them. The only explanation was that Kyle felt very sure of himself. In which case he was due for a shock.

Heat shimmered on the parking lot pavement. There was a strong smell of baking rubber. He unlocked the red Lincoln, thinking of what Joanne had said. She was right. He'd sat around this damn town for too long. A woman like Jo deserved more than a '65 Lincoln and a couple thousand dollars. Not even a couple thousand dollars, he remembered. The money he'd left with Aunt Daisy all this time was no longer intact. Say eighteen hundred. Jo needed more than that. Somehow the thought made Kyle's role as patsy less unpleasant to think about.

He eased himself behind the wheel and hooked on a pair of sunglasses. The baldheaded man had stopped at the gate. Jordan started his motor. There was no other way out of the lot. What happened now was anyone's guess. The agency used a variety of vehicles. Only last night a kid in a leather jacket had tailed him home on a Harley-Davidson. He eased the big sedan forward, irritated by the farcical aspect of the production. The charade had become pointless. It was only a matter of hours before Kyle would know of his defection. He braked on impulse at the gate and leaned his head through the window.

11

"Want a lift?" The baldheaded man was leaning against the wall behind a newspaper. Jordan called again. "You want a lift downtown?"

The man detached himself from the wall. He lowered his paper slowly and cleared his throat. He made no answer but spat. Jordan let the Lincoln glide a couple of feet nearer. He grinned. "It isn't a communist conspiracy. What's your problem?"

The session at the bar had left the man's face flushed. "Drop dead," he said sourly.

Jordan shook his head chidingly. "That's not nice, friend. I'm trying to save your shoe leather. I thought you'd like to know: I'm going straight back to the Casablanca Apartments. I'll take a shower there and change. I ought to make my aunt's place in Palamos by five o'clock. If I happen to see any one of you characters up there I'll run him down. Spread the word, will you?"

The man's flabbergasted expression stayed with Jordan as he took the Santa Monica freeway to the one north of Highland Avenue. A radio announcer cut in on the rhythm-and-blues program with a Sigalert. The bulletin warned of traffic congestion this side of Oxnard. He used the off-ramp at Barham Boulevard. The Casablanca Apartments lay behind the Warner Brothers Studio. The apartment building was a collection of mock-Moroccan bungalows badly in need of a face lift. He drove into his carport and cut the motor. He no longer cared whether anyone had tailed him. Tonight was going to be different from all the other nights. Tonight and the days that would follow — the years, maybe. Joanne and he had as much chance as anyone else.

The sun was low when he drove out of Palamos. An involuntary belch revived the taste of his aunt's weird cooking. Daisy Palumbo lived out of her store cupboard, blending the contents of cans haphazardly. Tonight's offering had been a near-lethal mixture of crabmeat, chili beans, and Tabasco. He shifted into drive and settled back. What little he remembered of his mother made comparison with her sister ridiculous. Aunt Daisy's idiosyncrasies were legend in the family. His mind ran through them indulgently.

She'd taken the highest honors of her class at U.C.L.A. and married a punch-drunk fighter out of Sausalito. Seven years later her husband had reversed a truckload of cement into the harbor and stayed there with it. Aunt Daisy collected his insurance and moved into the Communion of Saints, a cult village off Highway 101. She lived there alone now, drinking beer and bombarding her nephew with criticisms. She did her thwarted best somehow to replace her dead sister. Nuts, he decided. But nuts in the nicest way.

The miles flicked by monotonously. Pismo Beach. San Luis Obispo. It was still early evening. A haze obscured the oak-covered hills. Cattle ranged, bellowing with thirst. The next hours took him through truck-farming country, through a long level valley with mountains in the distance. He forked west at Salinas, skirting the Fort Ord military reservation. The fenced periphery and forbidding signs were reminders of an almost forgotten interlude in his life. Pfc. Jordan, draftee and nonhero. The streetlamps were lit when he drove into Pacific Ramparts. It was past nine. Another twenty minutes would see him in Las Rosas. Jo

13

was always punctual. He hesitated in front of the liquor store, wondering about champagne. He decided against it. The pot he'd promised to bring was in his pocket. They'd probably turn on and listen to music for a while before going to bed.

He drove out of town onto the hardtopped lane that linked Pacific Ramparts with the beach at Las Rosas. The pine trees at its end were black against a deep purple sky. The Lincoln nosed deep into cover, catching Joanne's convertible in its headlights. He cut them and walked to the fringe of the beach. White curls of surf were rolling toward the shore. The moon was a sliver of silver lying on its back. Lights were burning in the last but one beach house a couple of hundred yards distant. The warm air was fragrant with the distinctive smell of pine. He started toward the lights, his feet sinking in the still-warm sand. He could hear the record player going as he neared the Kyle place. The other houses were only used in the daytime. He stopped, hearing the sound of a car being started. He traced the noise to the bluff at the north end of the bay. There was a house there up among the cypresses. A dirt road gave it access to the highway a couple of miles out of town.

He plowed on through the loose sand to the back steps. He steadied himself there against the rails, shaking out one shoe after another. The porch extended on all four sides of the house. Lights shone from the living room windows facing the ocean. He ducked under a surfboard hanging from the rafters. It belonged to Kyle's daughter, a tall sullen-mouthed girl with sun-bleached hair. He'd once seen her driving with her father. He called Joanne's name softly. The noise of the record player drowned his voice. The patch

14

of light out front extended to the edge of the water. The screen door creaked gently in the breeze. The inner door was ajar.

He stepped inside, sniffing the burned-grass stink of marijuana. She'd turned on without even waiting for him. He was vaguely disappointed. The living room curtains were undrawn. Two small lamps burned in the window embrasures like beacons. He lowered the volume of the record player and called again. There was still no answer. She was probably in the bathroom. A fifth of Teacher's whisky stood on the table. The studio couch had been dragged away from the wall to face the ocean. The green scarf trailing from its end lifted in the current of air from the open door. His voice was sharper now.

"Jo?"

The Swingle Singers ended their Bach in a succession of diminishing chords. Apprehension gripped him like a vise. He half swung toward the bedroom, expecting to see a face smiling in the shadows. The record player stopped abruptly. There was no sound in the house. Nothing but the hammering in his chest and the distant roar of the breaking surf. He took five long steps to the bedroom. He pushed the door back gently and snapped on the light.

Joanne was lying on her back on the bed, her arms outstretched, staring at the ceiling. A snail of foam wormed its way from her left nostril as he watched. The window to the porch was open. He dropped on his knees by the side of the bed and took her wrist in his fingers. The flesh was warm but there was no pulse. He heaved himself up, his hands trembling. He just managed to make it to the bathroom. He leaned against the wall, sweat rolling down his back and face. Suddenly he started to retch violently. He continued till his voided stomach hurt. He stuck his head under the cold water faucet, walked back to the bedroom, and looked down at her through the salt sting of tears. Her swollen tongue was trapped between her teeth. It was too soon yet for death to bring calm to her features. He came out of his stunned bewilderment, his first thought to cover her body. One breast was protruding through the front of her silk lounging pajamas. He dropped the sheet, hearing footsteps on the porch outside. It was too late to switch off the light. He backed off into the passage. The footsteps on the porch stopped. He heard two men talking. One was vaguely familiar. The screen door burst open as he reached the living room. The first man in was built on the order of a middleweight, thickset with spread features under a ferocious bristle of black hair. His partner was the baldheaded man who'd been in the restaurant earlier. A 35mm camera was slung over his shoulder. He lifted a flash gun defensively at Jordan. His partner raised a leg. The door cracked shut. His hand streaked from the pocket of his sports jacket. The stubby barrel of a police special was pointing at Jordan's stomach.

Jordan's voice wavered. He pointed at the bedroom. "She's dead. Somebody's got to get help!"

The man in the loud shirt grinned. "Hear that, Al? The guy says we've got to get help."

An icy hand reached into Jordan's chest. "Now wait a minute," he began.

The man with the gun cut him short. "On your can, buster," he ordered in a hard flat voice.

16

Jordan lowered himself onto the couch. He lit a cigarette, doing his best to keep his hand steady. Confused anger raced in his mind. No more than minutes could have separated him from Jo's killer. The only cars in the pines had been hers and his. He was sure of it. Suddenly he remembered the sound of the motor up on the bluff. There was a way down to the beach. He loosened his shirt collar, imagining Kyle's slow descent. The Englishman's imposing figure would be menacing in the moonlight. Yet there was something wrong about the picture. The agency operatives had come with cameras, prepared for action. Maybe Jo hadn't said anything to Kyle at all. Maybe he'd just followed her to the beach. In which case there was no longer room for logic.

The baldheaded man grabbed the phone and dialed. He seemed to be enjoying himself. His voice took on an importance as his call was answered.

"Is this the Fairfax County Sheriff Department? Sheriff Kowalsky? This is Sy Barlow — from the Roscoe Agency in L.A., Sheriff. I'm calling from the Kyle beach house out at Las Rosas. Miss Kyle's dead, Sheriff. Yeah, strangled, by the look of her. We've got the guy right here." He sucked on a back tooth, wincing as the gravel-hard voice rasped into his ear. "Sure, Sheriff. You betcha. No, nothing's been touched. Half an hour'll be fine. Don't worry, he ain't going nowhere!"

His wink for Jordan was ironical. "You just got yourself some help! Hit him anywhere below the balls if he moves, Al!"

17

Brady Jordan   September 1969

HE GLANCED UP at the clock. It was twenty minutes of ten. They had brought him over to the courthouse from the county jail earlier than usual for some reason. The jurors were on their benches. There was nobody yet at the county prosecutor's table. He imagined the three men sitting in the Fairfax Hotel Coffee Shoppe: Abbott, Kowalsky, and Rahvis, the three vultures sharpening their beaks for the last day's work.

The jail presser had done a good job on his gray herringbone tweed jacket. He was wearing his last clean silk shirt and a black tie donated by his lawyer. Donatelli had an eye for detail and decorum. The spectator benches were already full. The Hollywood contingent had managed to hit the front as usual. Jordan recognized a couple of agents but not his own. The Negro girl from the Screen Writers' Guild had been busily taking notes throughout the trial. The woman in the full black veil and mourning clothes was in her customary seat directly behind the defense table. Donatelli said that she was an eccentric who covered every murder trial south of San Francisco. Her escort was a popeyed character who leaned forward, trying to attract Jordan's attention. He closed an eye in conspiratorial fashion and made a circle of solidarity with his thumb and forefinger. Jordan ignored him.

These were the worst moments — the long wait before Judge Sherman made his entrance. The jurors had moved into their accustomed huddles. The women were on the rear bench, the men in front. The foreman was a light-skinned Negro dentist. As far as Jordan could guess, the guy spent his time inspecting the bridgework of the witnesses. The machinery of the court was fully wound. Ten o'clock would set it in motion. Until then, apart from the clowns sitting behind him, there was a tacit agreement to ignore the defendant and his lawyer. It was just as well in view of their conversation.

Donatelli started it, coming out of his slump with a mournful look on his face. "Kyle's next on the stand. For the last time, Brady, I'm telling you I don't want to attack him. This kind of cross-examination gets us nowhere. We don't need it."

Jordan's expression set obstinately. "You may not — I do. I haven't spoken to the bastard since that night. I want to hear him answer those questions in open court."

The lawyer blew hard. "You already know what the answers will be. I know how the court'll see it. They'll see Kyle bending over his wife's coffin with you trying to stick a knife in his back. That's what."

Jordan affected an interest in his fingernails. "You've got a good line in metaphors, Counselor. But the knife's in *my* back not his. You're forgetting he set me up for murder."

The lawyer's hands moved expressively. "The evidence doesn't show it. Kyle won't admit it. What are we supposed to be trying to do — prove *he* killed his wife?"

Jordan had lain awake for too many nights in pursuit of the answer to precisely that question. Desolate hours with the drunks snoring away in the tank across the corridor.

"No," he said grudgingly. "Maybe not Kyle."

"Well thank God for that!" Donatelli said with feeling. A sprout of black hair joined his eyebrows in a straight bar. "I don't understand you, Brady. This isn't the detective room in a Los Angeles precinct. I'm a trial lawyer and Kyle's alibi is unassailable. The wife of a distinguished local resident is murdered. Query: Where was the said distinguished resident at the material time?"

Jordan glanced at him coldly. "Who do you think you are — Raymond Burr?"

Donatelli rode the interruption easily. "I'll tell you where he was: seventeen miles away. He says so. His daughter says so. His housekeeper says so. And it's the widow Bruce's testimony that puts a halo around Kyle's head. You saw her on the stand. She lives in fear of the Lord. That woman's incapable of telling a lie and everyone in this room knows it." Even with his voice at low register, his Adam's apple jumped and jerked. It was only one of a number of things about the lawyer that irritated Jordan. Donatelli was a composite of every farm boy who has hung up a shingle. He had the Abe Lincoln bang of hair and side whiskers, the deliberate choice of folksy idiom. He even moved like a hick when he was on his feet — creakily, as if his hands were gripping a pair of plow handles.

"I'm telling you Kyle knows who really killed his wife," Jordan said doggedly.

Donatelli sighed. "You're the one who's standing trial, Brady. Not Kyle or his daughter or his housekeeper."

Jordan poured himself a glass of water from the bottle on the table. It was flat and tasted of chemicals.

21

"They're laying five to one over in the jail that I finish in the gas chamber. You tell me those odds are crazy. I've *got* to believe you but I still want you to put those questions to him."

Donatelli had no chance to answer. Abbott, the county prosecutor, was making his way down the aisle. A man in a sheriff's uniform followed him. The third man in the group was a dried-out character carrying a small black bag. The beefy cop at the door lowered himself onto a canvas-backed stool. He thrust out his legs across the aisle, effectively barring further entry to the courtroom. Abbott's chunky figure filled his chair. He laughed suddenly, almost happily. Sunlight caught the gleam of gold in his mouth. Donatelli seemed immature in comparison, like a Boy Scout who has wandered into a poolroom.

There was a glimpse of ancient oak trees beyond the fly-screened windows. Jordan could see the couple of trusties from the jail, aimlessly pushing their brooms along the gutters. Old men were out in the early morning sunshine. The bench where they sat was immediately opposite the courthouse steps. They were old men in baseball caps and faded Levi's, unimpressed by the Hollywood-registered convertibles. All were indifferent to the man sitting fifty yards away on trial for his life. Kyle's Rolls was parked in front of the Fairfax Hotel. Somehow it was like the man himself — an old model, out-of-date but maintained with loving care and polished.

Jordan was careful not to turn his head. Kyle was somewhere behind next to his daughter. For no reason at all, Jordan found himself remembering Louella's classic quote.

The one that proved that she could even soar out of her own manic league on occasion: *Sebastian Kyle — the one director working capable of playing on the human heart as an instrument.*

Donatelli's urgent whisper chopped into Jordan's reverie. "For the last time, Brady. You heard what Weinberg told you last night. You're as good as on the street. Our testimony's going to blast Abbott out of his socks. I don't want you to do this to me, kid. I've put too much work into this case. Blood, sweat, and tears, let alone what it's cost me in fees."

"Blood, sweat, and tears," Jordan repeated ironically. "Crap. You've told me what it's cost you in fees nine times already. Or maybe it's ninety-nine. What are you bitching about? You've got yourself on the front page of every newspaper from here to Rahway, New Jersey. Ask the questions or I'll ask them myself."

It was two minutes to the hour. The jurors had assembled in their official places. The elderly woman in the Sears Roebuck hat closed her eyes as if praying for guidance. A buzzer sounded. The usher's bawl drowned out Donatelli's answer.

"Be upstanding for His Honor Judge Sherman!"

There was a general shuffling of feet. Jordan was already up, facing the door opening behind the rostrum. Sherman was a spare-boned bachelor in his late sixties given to the wearing of bow ties, a different one each day. The day's offering was blue silk polka dot. Sherman bowed and took his seat on the bench. Jordan suspected that the heavy-framed spectacles were an affectation. There had been

23

times when he had found the naked blue eyes fixed on him with stern appraisal. Sherman ruled his court firmly, making no concessions to the Hollywood contingent. He shifted the battery of pens on his desk and had a brief word with his clerk. The court reporter's fingers hovered over his stenotype machine. The judge's voice was quietly courteous.

"If you please, Mr. Abbott."

The prosecutor came to his feet with confidence. The pockets of his linen jacket sagged under the weight of his hands.

"Call Sebastian Kyle!"

Jordan poured himself another glass of water nervously. It was difficult to keep from turning his head. He heard the measured tread coming down the aisle. He imagined the look of dignified bereavement. Abbott moved toward his witness solicitously, shepherding Kyle to the stand. The Englishman took the oath in a quiet firm voice. Thirty years in the States had left his British accent unimpaired. He was a ponderous man with the top-heavy head of a Roman bust. Damp silver hair lay flat on his scalp. He wore a black band on the sleeve of his old-fashioned alpaca jacket. He sat down carefully and hitched himself closer to the microphone. His labored breathing sounded in the speakers. Abbott stepped sideways, allowing the jurors a clear view of his witness.

"Your full name is Sebastian Gibbons Kyle. You're a film director by profession, sixty-four years of age, and you reside at Oak Valley in the County of Fairfax. Is that correct, sir?"

Kyle signified assent. Jordan sneaked a look at him. The

witness was intent on his questioner. Donatelli was rattling his pencil between his teeth. Abbott strutted across to his table. He pulled a batch of glossy photographs from his dispatch case. Jordan averted his eyes. The pictures were macabre reminders of the night in May. He'd seen them all a dozen times before. Donatelli's papers concealed a set. Others were distributed among the jurors. Judge Sherman was reaching for his. Abbott's voice was charged with regret.

"I'm going to have to ask you to look at several of these pictures, sir. I'll take you back to the night of May 22nd, this year. At that time did you own a beach house situated at Las Rosas in the County of Fairfax?"

"I did. I still do."

"Can you tell us where you were about five minutes to ten on the night of May 22nd?"

"At home — in Oak Valley. My daughter and I had dined together. My wife was out. We were watching television when my housekeeper told me I was wanted on the phone."

The county prosecutor's glance at the jurybox was insinuating. "We've heard Sheriff Kowalsky say that he made that call from the beach house. Please tell the court what you did as a result of this message, Mr. Kyle."

The Englishman's voice faltered. "My daughter drove me to Las Rosas. I was in no condition, you understand." He regained his composure with an effort. "When we got there I saw the sheriff's car. Someone had turned a searchlight on the beach. We went inside. I saw my wife's body lying in the bedroom. Doctor Rahvis told me that she'd been strangled to death."

Abbott's expression identified him with the murmur of

25

sympathy that swept through the court. Judge Sherman rapped with his gavel. Abbott cleared his throat.

"Everyone here knows how you feel, Mr. Kyle. But I have to put these questions to you. I'll make them as brief as I can. Can you remember how many people were in the bedroom at that time?"

Kyle hung his head, thinking. "I'm not certain. Nine, I think."

"Try to remember who they were," Abbott invited.

Kyle's imposing head lifted. The look he shot at the defendant made no secret of his accusation. "Sheriff Kowalsky and two deputies. Doctor Rahvis, a couple of men from the Roscoe Agency, my daughter, Jordan, and myself."

Abbott dissolved into innocence. "Did Mr. Jordan's presence in the beach house come as a surprise to you?"

Kyle's cough rattled in the speakers. An usher turned the volume down. "No. That is, I knew that he and my wife had been seeing one another. I'd had reports from the detective agency. That's why the operatives were there that night."

"Tell us about that." Abbott leaned back, groping for the rail that separated him from the public benches. "We've heard the evidence of the operatives. They'd had your wife and the defendant under observation for some time, hadn't they? I'd like to have you tell the court how this came about."

Kyle brushed his hand across his eyes. The memory was obviously painful. "I'm afraid I employed them, sir. I had my reasons."

Abbott dropped his voice. "I have to put these questions to you, Mr. Kyle. I'm fully aware that you find them unpleasant. Isn't it the truth that you suspected your wife of having associations with other men?"

Kyle gripped the sides of the stand. "Other men, no. Jordan, yes. Is it really necessary to go into the intimacies of my life like this?"

"I'm afraid it is," Sherman interposed gently. "The court is deeply concerned with the pain these questions must be causing you but a man is on trial for his life. Answer the prosecutor, please."

"I have, Your Honor."

"Very well." Sherman put a question of his own. "What made you go to the detective agency, Mr. Kyle?"

The Englishman's performance riveted Jordan. It was worthy of an Academy Award. Kyle's chin came up. He met Sherman's look fairly. "I am sixty-four years of age, Your Honor. My wife was twenty-eight. The first year of our marriage was a happy one. I loved her then. I loved her at the moment of her death. But I would have been insane if I hadn't realized that something was going wrong between us. I noticed it first on my return from England last December. My wife seemed to be spending more and more time out of the house. It's difficult to explain how I felt. I suppose part of my brain wanted to accept the excuses she made for her endless absences. Perhaps it was because in a way I felt I was to blame. You see, I've worked in the motion picture industry for thirty-five years but I've always kept my private life apart. Joanne could never understand this. She even resented it. Everything Hollywood

27

stands for she admired. I started hearing rumors. That's when I went to the Roscoe Agency. I had to be sure — for my own peace of mind."

Abbott sidled nearer the jurors, taking up the examination again. "We've heard the testimony of the operatives concerned, the reports they made to you. The defendant was seen in the company of your wife on no less than thirty-odd occasions. The venues seem to have varied. Drive-in theaters, restaurants, studio parking lots. We also know that your wife met Jordan at the beach house six separate times. What did you do as a result of this information, Mr. Kyle?"

Sunshine slanted across Kyle's face. He brushed at it vaguely. It was some time before he answered. "Nothing, I'm afraid. At least, not at that time. It's like a man who's told that he has three months to live. Hope is sometimes stronger than the evidence. It's difficult for me to analyze my own motives then. I still loved my wife deeply, in spite of everything. I do know that I was ashamed of the part I was playing in the whole sorry mess. Secretly I hoped that there was still a chance for us. That's when I made up my mind, it was on the day that she died, ironically enough. I made up my mind that I'd tell Joanne everything that I knew — I mean about these affairs. I wanted to see if we couldn't right the things that had gone wrong. I never had the chance to do it." The last words were almost whispered.

Abbott shifted his body to face the defense table. "One last question, Mr. Kyle. There's been testimony that marijuana was found in your beach house. The butts of two smoked cigarettes. To the best of your knowledge had your wife ever taken drugs?"

"Absolutely not!" Kyle's splendid head moved forcefully. "She was a moderate social drinker, other than that morning."

Abbott's arm shot out with extended hand. "Your witness, Counselor."

Donatelli shambled across to the stand, dragging a forefinger around the inside of his collar.

"You've just told the court that you intended to have a showdown with your wife, Mr. Kyle. When did you make that decision?"

Kyle shifted his head out of the sunlight, blinking. "I've already said that. On the afternoon of the day she was killed. It might have even been the morning. I can't specify an hour."

Donatelli honed his voice. "That I can well understand. Your wife had been covering up her absences with lies for all these weeks, sleeping with a man in your beach house. A man whose name you knew from the start! What was so special about May 22nd, Mr. Kyle?"

The Englishman's poise was invulnerable. "I have done my best to explain, sir. It's true that I told the Roscoe Agency I suspected I had grounds for divorce. It's true that I knew that my wife was meeting Jordan on the night she was murdered. It is also true that I was ashamed. It was the last sordid piece of news that decided me. The agency people were going to Las Rosas that night with cameras. I remember that I thought about it for a long time that afternoon. It was six by the time I made my mind up.

29

I kept phoning the agency. I wanted to call the whole thing off. It was too late. All I was getting was the answering service."

Donatelli affected amazement. "But you *knew* where everyone was! Why not go to the beach house yourself? Why not confront your wife and her lover — appeal to their better feelings? Wasn't that what you'd had in mind?"

Kyle smiled patiently. "With all respect, Mr. Donatelli, I find that line of questioning naive. I'm by no means a young man and your client has a reputation for violence."

The lawyer's voice was shrill with indignation. "I move that response be stricken from the record, Your Honor. There is no evidence whatsoever that my client is a violent man."

Sherman glanced down from his dais. "Did the defendant ever offer you violence, Mr. Kyle — or to others in your presence?"

Kyle shook his head. "No, sir. But I've worked with him on two occasions. One heard rumors."

Sherman made a note. "Let the previous answer be stricken from the record."

Donatelli took off his jacket. Sweat patches showed on the back of his shirt. He draped his coat on the back of his chair. He shook his head in answer to Jordan's urgent whisper. He prowled back to the stand, looking like an alley cat that has scented fish in the garbage.

"You say that these suspicions started when you first came back from England. Isn't it a fact that you knew then that your wife had been having affairs with men? But she was too smart for you, wasn't she? You knew the defendant needed

30

money and you offered him five thousand dollars to seduce your wife and give you the evidence you needed for a divorce! That's the real truth, isn't it, Mr. Kyle!"

Sherman silenced the sudden babble with a swipe of his gavel. "If the people in the front rows cannot behave themselves, this court will rid itself of their presence."

Kyle's face was suddenly old and tired. He wet his lips. "I make that four questions at once, Counselor. The answer is no to all of them."

Jordan was sitting with his elbows on the table, watching Kyle's expression. He saw the telltale flicker. Surely the jury had to see it as well! The one thing that would have proved Kyle was lying was missing — the check. The memory of his first night in custody was still vivid. The long hours of interrogation, the endless cups of coffee. It was two o'clock in the morning when he'd picked his ace from the hole. He'd told them about the check. A couple of deputies had gone out to Oak Valley and searched the dead woman's bedroom. Nothing. No check — not even a loose floorboard.

Donatelli stared at his feet for a while. He shook his head as if the ways of the world bewildered him. "A man in need of money," he repeated. "A Hollywood writer though not a very successful one. Wasn't this the kind of man you knew your wife would go for, Mr. Kyle? You were offering him five thousand dollars and throwing a good-looking woman at him. What did he have to lose? He's being tried for murder, remember, not his morals."

Kyle half heaved himself out of his seat. "Your suggestions are insulting, sir, but I'm obliged to refute them. There's not a single word of truth in anything you've said."

Donatelli lifted his arms in a gesture of helplessness. "That's all." He resumed his seat, still shaking his head.

Jordan's whisper was savage. "What kind of a pitch was that? You had him on the hook and let him go!"

Donatelli mopped his neck, the ball of gristle in his throat jumping. "Can't you see he's got the sympathy of everyone in this room? You're the one who needs it, not him."

Abbott's re-examination soothed Kyle. The prosecutor took him back to the heart of the matter.

"Have you *ever* given money to the defendant, for any reason whatsoever, Mr. Kyle?"

"No, sir, I have not."

"Have you ever promised him any money?"

"Never."

"Thank you, Mr. Kyle."

Kyle's passage back to his seat brought him close to the defense table. He almost stopped as he passed, eyes hooded. Then he was gone. Jordan's hostile glare followed him back to his seat. The Englishman's daughter was sitting next to him. She was a tall girl with a ragged crop of hair bleached by sun and salt water. She was twenty-four or -five with a network of fine lines around the corners of her eyes. She met Jordan's stare impassively. Her eyes were her most distinctive feature. They were shell gray in color and flecked like a cat's. She put her mouth close to her father's ear. He nodded. Abbott approached the judge's rostrum.

"That concludes the case for the state, Your Honor."

Sherman glanced up at the clock. "I don't know what sort of order you had in mind for your witnesses, Mr. Donatelli. I prefer testimony to be given without interruption if possible. I'm thinking about the lunch recession."

Donatelli rose quickly. "The defense will only call two witnesses, Your Honor. The accused will not take the stand."

Sherman pinched his upper lip thoughtfully. "It's entirely a matter for you, of course. I'd have imagined in the light of your last cross-examination . . ."

It was Donatelli's moment. He employed it to full effect. He hitched his pants up, the plowboy versus the city slickers.

"There's something I'd like to get straight, Your Honor, with the court's permission. The defense certainly claims that Mr. Kyle connived at his wife's seduction. We make no secret of it but this is not our reply to the major indictment. My direct examination shouldn't take long and my feeling is that Mr. Abbott's going to need even less for his cross."

The county prosecutor yawned hugely. Sherman looked at the clock and sighed. "Very well. Call your first witness."

Donatelli shrugged off his opponent's supercilious grin. He turned to the usher. "Call Colonel Dempsey."

A lanky man with rimless spectacles strode from the back of the court. The top of his head looked as if it had been shorn with a lawn mower. No more than a yellow white stubble was left. He was wearing freshly pressed tans and a two-tiered bank of medal ribbons. He took the stand and covered his heart with his cap, looking at the furled flag behind the judge's rostrum. His affirmation crackled in the speaker.

"Vincent Dempsey, colonel in the United States Army, presently attached to the Pentagon, Washington."

Donatelli dropped a note in front of Jordan. The words were underlined with a felt pen. *Sherman's got his eye on you — watch it!* Jordan balled the piece of paper and threw it in the trash basket. The mechanics of memory were a mystery. He couldn't have thought of Dempsey in fourteen years yet suddenly it was all like yesterday: fatigue duties under a July sun with officers' wives wheeling through camp in their convertibles, bare armed, scented, and utterly unapproachable. The recollection gathered detail. Saturday nights in Monterey, the curtained gloom of the four cocktail lounges open to enlisted men. Dispirited waitresses with fallen arches, dropouts from the Hollywood dream, dispensed beer to kids on their way to die in Korea. He still remembered the feeling of guilt as the M.P.'s pushed their way through the door, their rawboned faces under white helmets. "Pass, soldier!"

Guilt had then been identified with the man on the witness stand. It was weird to find "Discipline" Dempsey charging out of the past to the rescue. Jordan pulled himself erect and smoothed his hair with nervous fingers.

Donatelli grinned ruefully. "You're going to have to make allowances for me, Colonel. I'm liable to foul up with the correct army terms. I'm a navy man myself."

Palms beat together softly in Jordan's brain. His lawyer's claim to comradeship was at the same time an acceptance of superior knowledge. Donatelli went on.

"Will you tell the court your rank, posting, and function in July of 1954, Colonel?"

Dempsey's manner implied that he could have accounted for every hour of his fifty-odd years. "I was captain in command of C Company, 4th Battalion, 21st Infantry Regiment, stationed at Ford Ord in this state. It was a training unit for officers and men proceeding overseas."

Donatelli pointed at the table. "Do you recognize the defendant?"

Dempsey snapped his answer, consulting the typewritten

sheet in his hand. "I do. Pfc. Jordan 8364728. He was in my command from March 11th through August 20th. That would be 1954."

"A little more than five months," Donatelli remarked conversationally. "Would that be the usual period of training in this outfit, Colonel?"

The question appeared to surprise Dempsey. He hitched the upper half of his body to attention. "That would depend, sir. Specialists needed a longer period of training than others. Basic training for an infantryman at that time was three months."

The lawyer took a turn to the front row of jurors. "Was the defendant being trained as a specialist, Colonel?"

"He certainly was not," Dempsey said flatly.

Donatelli affected misunderstanding. "But he was with you for five months — how was that?"

The colonel wiped his spectacles before replying. "War or peace you always get the odd man who doesn't want to soldier. Some of them register as conscientious objectors. A fair percentage settles down under discipline. Others spend their wars in military prisons. The worst headache the army has is with malingerers."

Donatelli put him at ease. "I think we all understand that, Colonel. It's the same in any service. You'll always get the odd man who doesn't want to soldier — the bum who's ready for someone else to fight for his wife and sister. What I'm trying to establish is why Jordan's basic stretched from three into five months."

"There were good reasons," Dempsey said in a tight voice.

Donatelli took a paper from his pocket. He gave it to Sherman to look at. "This is a certificate of discharge from the

35

United States Army, Your Honor. In the name of the defendant and dated August 22nd, 1954."

He waited till the judge had done with the form then gave
it to the county prosecutor. Abbott waved it aside impatiently. Donatelli grinned at him. "I'd like this entered as an
exhibit, Your Honor." Sherman inclined his head. The
usher stuck a tab on a cellophane wrapper. Donatelli followed its progress to the usher's table and turned to Dempsey.

"I understand that the defendant was still under your
command when he was discharged, Colonel. I guess you'd
know the reasons — I mean why the army let him go."

Dempsey's amusement showed itself in a ripple of skin
above his ears. "Let him go? Jordan was left-handed. He'd
strip a carbine back to front. I never knew if it was done on
purpose or not. The point is I even had him salute me left-
handed. You can't have that sort of thing in the service. Left-
handed!"

Abbott had gone into a huddle with the county medical officer. Sheriff Kowalsky stepped over the restraining rail and
joined them at the table. The defense lawyer ignored the
interruption.

"I see what you mean, Colonel. You thought the defendant
was goldbricking, right?"

"Right," said Dempsey. "His general attitude made it
probable. Jordan's contempt for discipline came through
loud and clear. He thought he was a cut above everyone
else. Smarter. He was never up on a charge, for instance.
That's the way I had it figured, anyway." The habit of command was strong and he made no apology.

Jordan's expression was unchanged. His mind was back
in the plank-floored hut. The color of Dempsey's crew cut

had changed since then but nothing else. They'd been alone in Dempsey's office. He could still hear the other man's snarled threat. "I'm throwing you to the head shrinkers, soldier. God help you if you don't come up swimming."

The defense attorney took the colonel along smoothly. "A cut above everyone else, you said. Smarter. In fact, as far as you were concerned, this left-handed business was no more than an act, wasn't it, Colonel? An act designed to get Jordan out of serving his country? You couldn't let him go overseas the way he was, so what happened?"

Dempsey shrugged. "There *was* only one thing to do — put him in front of a medical board. They had him under observation for five weeks and recommended a discharge. I'm told there's a technical term to describe his condition. I'm not even going to try and remember it."

"We'll hear more about that in good time," Donatelli promised. "The fact is, my client was examined by a medical board appointed by the United States Army, men qualified to adjudicate in such matters. They found that Jordan uses his left hand as others use their right — correct?"

"Correct." Dempsey peered across the court at the defendant. The inspection seemed to afford little satisfaction.

Donatelli lacked a cape but the movement was that of a bullfighter — the pirouette held, stomach sucked in, chin held up. "Your witness, Mr. Prosecutor."

Some of Abbott's confidence seemed to have leaked away. He still managed to go at Dempsey as a terrier does at a rat. "How many types of discharge are there in the United States Army, Colonel?"

Dempsey answered with authority. "Three: honorable general, and dishonorable. Jordan went out on a general."

Abbott bounced a meaningful look along the front line of jurors. "It's plain enough what the first and last terms indicate. How about the second — the one you say Jordan went out on?"

Dempsey glanced up at the judge. "That would depend on the circumstances, Your Honor. The army's always ready to give a soldier a break. A dishonorable discharge bars a man from all benefits. We don't use it unless the case is a flagrant one."

Abbott jumped him immediately. "In other words, the medical board was giving the defendant the benefit of the doubt."

Dempsey balled his shoulders. "I don't know. I wasn't on the board."

Abbott kicked away the answer like a hockey player minding his net. "Let's put it another way, Colonel. There's a type of soldier that's expert in fooling medical boards. I guess you've seen plenty of this, all the years of service you've put in."

Dempsey's tone was acid. "It wouldn't be the sort of thing I'd talk about if I had."

Abbott's face reddened. "Let me remind you that you're a witness under oath, Colonel. Answer the question in a proper manner."

Dempsey's lips moved. Sherman's intervention halted the heated exchange.

"One minute, Mr. Prosecutor. I heard the witness's answer though I doubt if anyone else did. You're shouting. The answer to your question was 'no.'"

Abbott called it a day and joined the others at his table. He was plainly shaken. Rahvis and Kowalsky were rifling through the morgue shots. The medical examiner's fingers were flying agitatedly. Donatelli was wearing his secret smile.

"Call Doctor Benjamin Weinberg."

A small, neatly dressed man came down the aisle. He covered his head and took the oath with a Brooklyn accent. Jordan watched him with a hope that Donatelli had never been able to inspire. The lawyer hooked his thumbs in his belt loops and spread his legs. "Will you state your qualifications, Doctor?"

Weinberg folded his short arms. His voice was pleasant and completely without pretentiousness. "I graduated at Columbia and the Sorbonne and I hold a degree from Duke University. All three degrees are in the field of medicine."

Donatelli registered respect. "Thank you, Doctor. And you practice in New York City. Is that as a specialist or as a general practitioner?"

"I am a forensic consultant." Weinberg blew his nose and smiled at the judge.

Donatelli inclined his body toward the jurors. "Have you made a special study of death by strangulation, Doctor?"

"I have."

Donatelli pursed his lips. "Maybe you'd tell the court how many times you've appeared as an expert witness where death was caused by strangulation. Would it be ten — twenty?"

Weinberg lifted himself on his toes. "I believe this is to be the one hundred and seventh occasion. My secretary would know for sure."

"And always for the defense?"

Weinberg signified denial. "Rarely for the defense, sir.

In fact this is only the fifth time. This I can be sure about. You see it's the state that always seems to have the money."

Sherman rapped down the ripple of laughter. "The witness will confine himself to answering the questions."

Donatelli was completely undisturbed. Jordan noticed that several of the jurors had smiled, including the foreman.

"Perhaps you'd give us a general description of death by strangulation, Doctor Weinberg, remembering that we're laymen."

There was a sudden hush, an air of expectancy. Jordan kept his eyes on the little doctor. Weinberg blew his nose hard again before answering.

"Strangulation is a constriction of the neck, manual or otherwise. The end result has the effect of cutting off the breathing and the supply of blood to the brain. Any number of factors can modify the situation but those are the basic facts."

"They'll do," said Donatelli, shooting a glance at his adversary. The county prosecutor was cleaning his pen. Rahvis looked considerably more concerned. He cocked his head as his name was mentioned. "You've heard Doctor Rahvis's testimony as to the cause of death. You've seen the pictures taken in the morgue ten hours afterward. Do you find any discrepancy here at all?"

Weinberg nodded briskly. "Yes I do. The digital bruises that appear in the photographs are not mentioned in the addendum to the death certificate. That is, Doctor Rahvis's list of general injuries to the dead woman."

"Can you think of any reason why that should be?"

"There are several. The most likely is that the certificate

was issued shortly after death was ascertained. The bruises I'm referring to wouldn't have shown at that time."

Donatelli gave the witness one of the morgue shots. "I'd like you to point out those bruises for the jurors, Doctor."

Weinberg did so, holding up the photograph. His finger traced across the dead woman's neck. Jordan looked away quickly.

"These are the imprints of a thumb and forefinger. There are other prints on the right side of the neck but these are barely discernible. There is a general area of bruising. This I would expect. An assailant's hands shift during the struggle. Now starting at the top of the subject's head we can just note a two-inch scalp wound. This would probably be caused by a blow or a fall before she collapsed on the bed. The face and forearms show traces of scratching. The marks are superficial. There's a deeper scratch on the left nipple."

"Tell us a little more about these injuries," Donatelli invited. "Which of them would be hidden when the body was found?"

"The wound in the scalp very probably. Some of the scratches and of course the digital bruising on the throat." Weinberg returned the photographs to the lawyer.

Defense counsel threw it on the table. "Am I right in assuming that in a struggle of this kind between adults, mutual injuries are always inflicted?"

"That's correct. If the victim is a woman she tends to defend herself by biting and scratching."

"That is to say that in a murder of this type, you'd expect to find the assailant pretty well marked up?"

"I'd find it difficult to accept any other conclusion, Coun-

selor. A tall man might be able to defend his face to some
extent but he'd almost certainly be marked. Of course, some
of the traces might be hidden by his clothing. There's no
question in my mind that this woman put up a determined
struggle for her life."

"A determined struggle." Donatelli dwelt on the words.
He handed Weinberg another photograph. "Here's a picture of the defendant taken in the nude forty-five minutes
after his arrest. We had it done with the permission of the
sheriff. It naturally blocked any false charges of police
brutality that might be made subsequently. It turns out to
have further significance. The only extraneous mark showing on his body at that time was an inch-and-a-half ap-
pendectomy scar that was fifteen years old. Does this surprise you?"

"Viewed in the light of the charge against him it astonishes me."

"You are an expert witness called by the state on no fewer
than one hundred and two occasions and you say that this
astonishes you, Doctor! Have you formed any opinion about
how the dead woman *was* strangled?"

"Yes, I have. She was strangled from the front and by
a right-handed man. The latent digital bruising would
strongly support this theory."

"A *right*-handed man — you're sure about that, Doctor?"

Weinberg's shoulders lifted. "It's an area in which there
can be no certainty, Counselor. But I'd be willing to
bet on it."

"Objection!" Abbott was up on his feet, red-faced and
hoarse. "We're not interested in the witness's gambling pro-
clivities, Your Honor."

Weinberg was not to be beaten down. "I am ninety percent certain that the murderer was right-handed, Your Honor. I base this opinion on the all-important positioning of the digital imprints. If the court will allow me, I'd like to demonstrate."

Sherman waved a hand. Weinberg came down from the stand. Jordan had already seen the maneuver rehearsed. It was nonetheless impressive. Weinberg was a head shorter than the defense attorney. He rose on his toes, gripping Donatelli by the throat. He might have been addressing a class of students.

"Observe the bias as I apply pressure. Notice how my right shoulder comes forward fractionally. This is because I'm generating more power on this side. Each of us is stronger in one arm than in the other. If I happened to be sinistro-manual — that's left-handed — the bias would be on the other side."

He took his fingers away from Donatelli's neck. The attorney massaged his neck theatrically. Weinberg took his place on the stand again. The jurors were watching his every move. Donatelli's face was suddenly somber.

"The defense has produced irrefutable evidence that my client is left-handed. He has been so since birth. An hour after his arrest, state authorities stripped him naked as the day he was born. They photographed him in this condition as prescribed by law. *Not one single sign of a struggle was found on his body.* I ask you now for your considered opinion, Doctor. *Could* Jordan have committed this crime?"

Weinberg was quietly positive. "In my opinion, no."

Sherman beat Donatelli to the next question. "You've enlightened us considerably with regard to certain matters,

43

Doctor. Can you think of any reason why these discrepancies you spoke of should have been overlooked elsewhere?"

"I take it you want more than a 'yes' or 'no' on this occasion, Your Honor?" Weinberg's tone was mildly sarcastic.

Sherman's hand covered a fleeting smile. "In this case, yes."

Jordan was conscious of scrutiny from the jurors' bench. A woman in the back row was whispering to the foreman who turned and nodded emphatically. Weinberg sat with tightly folded arms, impregnable to any assault on his beliefs.

"My feeling is that the reason here is obvious, Your Honor. A man is found standing over the body of a strangled woman. There's an a priori assumption that he's responsible for her death. I would say that the rest stems from this one fact — an overhasty assessment of guilt."

Sherman made a notation as Donatelli moved in swiftly. "I've lived in a small community all my life. I've had the privilege of seeing county medical examiners at work. For the most part, they're dedicated men struggling with large private practices. Isn't it a fact that a man like this would tend to be tired at the end of the day?"

Abbott rocketed up. His face was flushed and combative. "Objection. The witness isn't a county medical examiner. The question is immaterial and irrelevant."

"But not incompetent," Sherman said drily. "The question calls for an opinion in an area in which the witness is expert. Objection overruled."

Weinberg's glance at the prosecution table made no secret of his contempt. "I'd say a man like that would be tired, yes. I find it a little strange that the local authorities ordered no autopsy. Maybe they were all tired."

"Your witness." Donatelli took his place beside Jordan.

Abbott's face had turned a much paler shade of tan. He looked like a fighter who is waiting for the bell to save him. He walked slowly to the stand and snapped one question after another.

"There's no such thing as a completely and compulsively left-handed person, is there, Doctor?"

"Phrased like that, no."

"Just as no one's completely right-handed?"

"Correct."

"Since a left-handed person lives in a world geared for the right-handed he's generally more ambidextrous?"

"I'm replying now to the generalization. Yes."

"Are you telling the court that it would have been impossible for the accused to have committed this murder, Doctor?"

"Impossible, no. But highly improbable."

Abbott threw up his hands and registered disgust. "That's all, Doctor."

Donatelli waived the right to re-examine. "The defense rests, Your Honor."

A glacial silence reigned as Weinberg made his way back to his seat. He walked like a pigeon, a ridiculous plume of hair nodding at the back of his head. He resumed his place to an outburst of congratulation. The jurors had drawn together, unnoticed in the general upheaval. They withdrew to their room. It was no more than a couple of minutes before the bailiff was summoned. He returned with a note that he handed to Sherman. The judge adjusted his spectacles and read the slip of paper. He turned his head, watching the door to the jury room. He waited till the twelve had

45

filed out and were back in their seats. His expression was impassive as he spoke.

"Ladies and gentlemen, I understand that you have heard enough evidence to arrive at your verdict?"

The foreman was on his feet. "We have, Your Honor. The verdict is 'not guilty.'"

"And is that the verdict of you all?" probed Sherman.

The dentist's voice cracked self-consciously. "It is, Your Honor."

Jordan felt the pressure of Donatelli's knee. He poured himself another glass of water and drank thirstily. Sherman made a neat pile of his papers. It was impossible to guess what lay behind the pale blue eyes.

"Let that verdict be so recorded," he said and turned to the jury. "Thank you, ladies and gentlemen. If you want to stay on, you may. It's entirely up to you. I would have thought that some fresh air would do us all good."

Abbott pulled himself together. "There's still the second count on the indictment, Your Honor — possession of three quarters of an ounce of marijuana.

Donatelli was up with him. "The defendant requests the court's permission to change his plea to one of 'guilty' on this count, Your Honor."

One of the wings of Sherman's bow tie was caught in his robe. He seemed to be unaware of it. His glance sought Abbott who inclined his head.

"Very well," said Sherman. "We don't have to go into all that again. The facts are in evidence. Is there anything you want to say before I pass sentence, Mr. Donatelli?"

Jordan watched the judge's eyes half close as the defense

attorney cleared his throat. Jordan listened to his lawyer like a man waking from a bad dream. The jurors had stayed in their places. The expressions on their faces reassured him that he wasn't dreaming as Donatelli droned on. The attorney dredged the past to color the image of his client. A childhood deprived of the guidance of parents — the promise offered by a brilliant university record. And so on. The stock phrases rolled into his peroration.

". . . the stresses and strains of the sort of life he led. This man has been punished enough for the offense to which he now pleads guilty. Justice must truly be done, Your Honor. We say, let it be tempered with mercy."

He strode back to the table and signaled Jordan to stand. Sherman leaned forward, washed blue eyes resting on the prisoner.

"I don't propose to waste too much time on you, Jordan. I've been watching you closely throughout this trial and I think I know what Colonel Dempsey had in mind. You do appear to be contemptuous of those you feel to be less gifted than yourself. However, I've tried to put this out of my mind when formulating your sentence. You will go to prison for no less than one and no more than two years as directed by the state of California — Youth and Adult Corrections Agency."

He collected his papers, ducked his head, and vanished through the door behind him. Sunshine flooded the rear of the court. The cop was opening the exits. Abbott came over, his savage undertone was for Donatelli not Jordan.

"Congratulations, Counselor. You should be proud of yourself."

The defense attorney looked him up and down. "What's your hang-up, Abbott? Next time the county tries railroading an innocent man may I suggest a little more homework?"

The courtroom was already half empty. The doors were open. Jordan could see Dempsey and Weinberg conversing in the lobby. Kyle was getting up from his seat. There was no way for him to avoid looking at the men at the defense table. He came to a halt as he reached the aisle, no more than six feet away. His big head slued around. His daughter was close behind him. Both of them glanced at Jordan as if they expected him to say something. The accused man smiled deliberately, holding the smile till both were out of sight in the lobby. He heard a hiss and turned.

The woman lifted her veil, showing a slashed mouth in a dead white face. She spoke in a deep contralto. "God knows the secrets of the human heart."

"Let her go," Donatelli said hastily. "She's a nut."

Sheriff Kowalsky's bulk loomed over them. "Let's wrap it up, Counselor. They want him across the street."

Donatelli shoved a cigar at him and lit one himself. He slipped into his jacket.

"Well there it is, Brady, just the way I said it would be. A few months in the pokey and you'll be back in business. Which reminds me, there's still a little cash outstanding." He picked a shred of tobacco from his lip and stared hard at it.

The courtroom was empty now except for the three of them — Kowalsky, Donatelli, and Jordan. Cigar smoke hung thick in the exhausted air.

"Which reminds you," Jordan repeated ironically, "you quoted a figure. Don't say you haven't had value."

Donatelli's bony shoulders rose and fell. "This amount doesn't appear on the expense account. It's only peanuts anyway — a couple hundred bucks. We had to pay your bill at the Casablanca Apartments before they'd release your things."

Jordan waved aside the proffered cigar case. The last of the vultures was waiting for his pickings.

"You ought to have the papers to a Lincoln convertible locked up in your safe. It used to be mine, now it's yours. I think I've got about eighteen hundred dollars left in the world. I need those to fight the good fight. I think you'll have to sue me for those two bills, Counselor."

Donatelli's laugh was entirely for Kowalsky. He doubled his fist and rapped Jordan with it lightly.

"Ah, forget it. That kind of money isn't going to make or break me. I'll make you a present of it. And watch yourself in there, hear now?"

Kowalsky broke it up. Jordan followed him down the aisle, out through the lobby, and down the courthouse steps. The square was strangely quiet. Most of the parked cars were gone. A few dogs lay under the trees, sheltering from the fierce noonday heat. The old men were still on their benches. Their heads lifted as Kowalsky passed with his charge. The sheriff waved greeting. One of the gaffers cackled. Jordan made the short walk with a sense of anticlimax. If he'd been found guilty the whole town would have been there licking its chops, sniffing the smell of death. Bastards.

Kowalsky waddled rather than walked. His belly overflowed his belt by a couple of inches. He shifted his mashed cigar.

"Left-handed, huh? Who dreamed that one up? Sure fooled the jury."

He took the cigar from his teeth and spat expressively. The gesture was a distant tip of the hat to a shrewd maneuver. It was obvious that Kowalsky still thought that Jordan was guilty.

"You can't win 'em all," said Jordan.

The cliché seemed to impress Kowalsky for some obscure reason. He nodded heavy agreement. "That's right, too."

He stopped in front of the mellowed brick building. He surveyed it with a kind of proprietorial interest. The upper windows were sealed by bars. Except for this the jail resembled the other houses on the square. Abbott lived in one, the county medical examiner in another. Wide steps led up to a tall-ceilinged hall. The floorboards were bare. A steel grille divided the lock-up area from the warden's living quarters. A combined smell of cooking and disinfectant soured the air. Kowalsky rattled his handcuffs on the bars. A vinegary voice answered the summons. A long thin man in tan slacks and shirt appeared, swinging a bunch of keys. He unlocked the gate in the grille. The sheriff herded Jordan through. His tone held a sort of reluctant admiration.

"The kid beat it, Joe."

The gate hack was unimpressed. "I heard. Bumpeye came running across the square right after the verdict, as fast as a coon will run. Charley Abbott's ass is gonna be real sore." He neighed high in his nose.

Neither man bothered to look at Jordan. "That's too bad,"

said Kowalsky. He leaned against the bars. "I'll be back for him after dinner. Don't forget to have his things ready." He lumbered out to the square.

The guard ran his hands lightly over Jordan's pockets. "You got anything on you, feller? No wise guy slip you anything in the courthouse?"

Jordan shook his head. "Just what I took with me, Joe."

The guard's eyes were satisfied. "OK. You want to go back to your cell or you want to go in the tank with Swenson?"

"I'll take the cell," said Jordan.

There was a small jail count except for Rodeo Week and Saturday nights. There were only three other prisoners besides Jordan. Two of them were trusties who swept out front, trimmed grass in the backyard, and cleaned the corridors. The third was an obstinate hulk named Swenson. The Swede was a repairman with the Pacific Gas and Electric Company and had himself hauled in once a year for nonpayment of alimony. The smell of cooking came from the warden's quarters. His wife catered for the prisoners and specialized in Spanish rice.

"Where's Kowalsky taking me?" Jordan asked suddenly.

The hack paused on the stairs, nursing his breath. "Springfield," he wheezed. "You got a break, first offender and all. I hear they even got visiting facilities for married men." He lingered with the word salaciously.

The man's neighing laugh was like sandpaper on Jordan's frayed nerve ends. There must be something about him that even an old goat like this recognized. He seemed to have trailed it all his life — a lure to women, an affront to other

51

men. But only a certain type of woman. The line had formed on the right, an anonymous amalgam of desire and pulchritude. He'd always liked them to be lookers. All of them were bent on the same thing. First came surrender and then possession. He'd lopped the line one after another, avoiding the trap with as much grace as they allowed. Carhops and continuity girls, Las Vegas matrons on temporary leave-of-absence from the marriage service — this was till he'd met Jo. Looking back, it was ironical.

The gate hack moved his feet wearily. His mind was on other matters.

"Let's go. It's almost noon already."

The second story had been gutted on conversion. Half a dozen cells were spaced around a central tank and separated by a corridor. Saw-proof steel bars extended from floor to ceiling. The walls of the jail were made of brick. Each cell had its wash basin, water spigot, and toilet. The iron beds were bolted to the ground.

Jordan's cell overlooked the square. By putting the stool on the bed and then standing on it he had a precarious view of the back of the courthouse and the taxi office. Kids played under the trees those dusty summer evenings. As the shadows grew longer, the Venuti family sallied out to throw bocci-ball in defiance of City Ordinance 38. Later came the sound of music, saturating the square till the cocktail lounge in the Fairfax Hotel closed down for the night. He'd been able to identify every noise, trace every humdrum happening in his imagination. This floor had been his home for sixteen weeks. Now it was over.

A propeller fan in the ceiling wafted tired air through the

cell-block. There were four shower stalls in a recess, a gas burner for brewing coffee. Swenson was lying on his belly in the tank, clad in his shorts. The line of deep tan stopped at his collar. His arms looked as if he were wearing brown elbow-length gloves. He came out of his crumpled newspaper, heaving himself up on one hand. Baby yellow hair grew in lank strands. He wrinkled his bright blue eyes at Jordan.

"Come over here and let me rub your hump. You should've took that bet, Brady. I hear old Doc Rahvis got to go back to school!"

The guard unlocked Jordan's cell, his voice sour. "If it's luck you're talking about, Swede, you're gonna need all you can get. Your crew's working out at Loner Lake. Those guys are coming in every night crippled with poison ivy."

Swenson scratched himself comfortably. "The hell with the P.G. and E. I've got another two weeks with you people. You see the warden's wife, Joe, tell her I changed my mind about dinner. I'd like a T-bone steak with French fries and a tossed salad on the side. And tell her to send up a couple of cold beers for me and my friend."

The guard thought about it long enough for Swenson to grin. Then he scowled. "You run your mouth too hard." He trailed the bunch of keys along the bars and disappeared.

Swenson came up expectantly. "Did you get it?"

Jordan flopped on the bed. "No."

"Why in hell not?" Swenson's expression was puzzled. "I told you what to do. All your lawyer needed was to drop the bottle in your pocket. You know Hank never searches properly coming back from the courthouse."

Jordan looked at him through two sets of bars. "I had

53

other things on my mind." The jail was trapped in the glare of the midday sun. In spite of the fan it was stifling in the cell-block. He took off his shirt.

Swenson scratched the hairs on his forearms. "You're the damnedest guy I ever saw. This lousy county sets you up for murder and you sit there looking like they pinned a medal on you. Don't *nothing* ever move you?"

"I'm like you, Swede. Immune to the slings and arrows."

His two bags were downstairs somewhere, his possessions listed in the guard's fourth-grade handwriting. One yellow metal watch. One yellow metal propelling pencil. They had a block about describing articles as gold. An operator's license and Social Security card. A leather wallet that had contained two hundred and forty dollars at the time of his arrest. Cigarettes and newspapers had exhausted most of this. Aunt Daisy's food packages had been for the most part inedible. The eighteen hundred bucks he had left with her was his entire bankroll. It was over two years ago, a clear day in April. He'd driven straight to Palamos from Vegas, barely able to keep his eyes open after an all-night stand at the dice table. Every gambler ought to have a night like that at least once in his life. To feel the squares of bone in his hand, roll them, and *know* how they'd land. He'd thrown eleven mains in a row and come out into the dawn forty-two hundred dollars ahead. Aunt Daisy had fed him coffee and a nonstop flow of contradictory advice. Gambling wasn't only immoral, it didn't make sense. This time he ought to use the money sensibly. By nine o'clock he'd given up, turning over half his winnings to her for safekeeping and sleeping the clock around. Aunt Daisy had sat on the loot for twenty-one months, resisting his demands for its return. Only once she had weakened, surrendering a couple hundred bucks to bail him out of a backlog of traffic violations.

He yawned and came back to the bars. "You know anything about the parole system, Swede?"

The blond giant pulled a sour face. "You putting me on? What in hell would I know about the parole system? Every time Sam Benurian gets me in front of him, he hits me with the book. Ninety days and this bit about a man's duty to support his wife. He shoulda lived with mine."

"You've been coming here for years," Jordan insisted. "You must have heard the guys talking — the old-timers. How's it work — what's the earliest I can hit the street on a one-to-two sentence?"

Swenson used his fingers to work it out. "Nine months, way I hear it. Two thirds of the minimum. And they tell me the parole board has to be real proud of you before they turn you loose. Know what, Brady, you're gonna have to be salutin' for your breakfast? You're gonna have to keep talking all about that good life you wanna lead."

A rattling of cans came from the staircase. A Negro trusty with a cauliflower ear and callused eyebrows appeared carrying two trays. He pushed one at each of them, through the slots in the bars.

"Now y'all eat up good," he admonished. "Miz Muller's worried you people ain't enjoying your food." He turned to Jordan, his dark face split in a delighted grin. "She-et, man, you *really* flyin'!"

There was a mess of rice, green peppers, and meatballs on the trays. A few prunes slopped in pale brown juice. The coffee in the paper cups was unsweetened. Swenson stuck his thumb in the rice and tasted it judiciously.

"She's light on the salt again," he complained. "Tell her this ain't what I ordered, Bumpeye."

"Light on the salt?" Bumpeye rested his chin on the bars, looking at Swenson with sad dignity. "You know what Miz Muller tole me, Swede? She tole me you're full of crap. Miz Muller's own words." He fished a cigarette from the pack with his gleaming teeth and addressed Jordan. "Joe wants you dressed and ready by two o'clock, Brady. The sheriff's gonna haul your ass outa here at two o'clock precisely." It was a new word and he repeated it. "Precisely!"

Swenson stared after him, shaking his head. He spoke with his mouth full. "That Bumpeye sure breaks me up!"

He was speaking to himself. Jordan was picking at the rice listlessly, thinking about Kyle's parting look as he had left the courtroom. The Englishman had dropped his guard for all to see during that brief second. He'd put a gun to a man's head and pulled the trigger. Boom-boom. Only the corpse had sat up again. Only one thing would be on Kyle's mind at the moment — that his safety would last as long as Jordan's sentence. Every day that ticked off the calendar was going to bring him closer to retribution. He knew it. Maybe he'd share the thought with whomever had killed his wife.

Jordan scraped the rest of the food into the toilet bowl and flushed it away. If Swenson was right and he used his head he'd be out in nine months. Nine months to produce a plan to avenge Jo's death. It wouldn't be easy. He had a feeling that nothing was going to be easy anymore. He and Jo had never had their chance together. But the emptiness he was left with was just as real as though they had. What did a man like Sherman know about love — or Abbott or Kowalsky! Whatever they felt was governed by statutes and conventions. Nothing would be right or real for them unless it bore the Good Housekeeping seal. Kyle was something else again. Kyle understood only too well.

He pulled on his pants and knotted his tie. Keys were jangling below. The guard appeared, short winded and testy. He unlocked Jordan's cell.

"All right, let's roll."

Jordan pushed a spare carton of cigarettes through the bars of the tank. Swenson cocked a lazy eye.

"Remember what I told you, Brady. Make that salute real happy. You ever hit this godforsaken town again you'll find me out at El Ranchero most nights. Route 28. See you."

He was asleep before they reached the stairs. Sheriff Kowalsky was waiting on the outside of the grille, picking his teeth. Handcuffs dangled from his belt. Jordan's bags were at the sheriff's feet.

"You oughta open up those goddamn skylights in here, Joe," he complained. "Place smells more like a pig farm every day."

"It's your breath blowing back in your face," the guard retorted with satisfaction. He gave Kowalsky a large envelope. "Here's his stuff."

Jordan signed the property register and carried his bags out to the white Dodge. A searchlight was fixed to the roof. The door panels bore the gold insignia of the Fairfax County Sheriff Department. The courthouse square drowsed in the heat. Someone in Dr. Rahvis's house was practicing scales erratically. Kowalsky settled himself in the driver's seat. Jordan came in beside him. Kowalsky unhooked the pair of cuffs from his belt.

"Gimme your left foot, Brady."

He slipped a steel loop around Jordan's ankle and fastened the free end of the manacles to the seat support. Jordan looked at the maneuver disbelievingly.

"What is this, some sort of joke, Sheriff? Where do you think I'm going, anyway?"

"When I'm sure I'm still not certain," Kowalsky grunted. The smell of beer was strong on him. He rolled down the window and switched on the radio. He drove slowly around the square, beating time on the steering wheel.

Route 28 wound through the valley fruit farms. Jordan was seeing it all as if for the first time. The soft dirt roads led up to neat Dutch barns, heavy-laden apple trees. Birds wheeled in the cloudless sky. The sheriff whistled tonelessly to the whining country music. A roadside shingle read

EL RANCHERO
DANCING EVERY SATURDAY NITE

Swenson's dream was a timbered shack with a mountain of empty bottles behind it. A Highway Patrolman wheeled out of the shade and zoomed after them. His image in the rearview mirror grew larger till at last he was alongside. Everything about him was outside and sinister — machine, sunglasses, and pistol. He took a hand from the wheel and waved. Kowalsky waved back and the cop gunned away,

58

the staccato sound of his exhaust splitting the quiet of the orchards.

Jordan shook his head again, not trusting himself to speak. Kowalsky allowed himself a rusty smile.

"I like to keep things tidy. You already made a fool outa me a coupla times."

He took his eyes from the road momentarily. A cutoff to the left climbed a rise, disappearing in a dense stand of oak trees. The house that lay behind them was out of sight. A sign was attached to the mailbox at the driveway entrance.

OAK VALLEY   PRIVATE PROPERTY   KEEP OUT

Kowalsky blinked as if hit from behind and suspended his whistling. "What in hell made you pull that crazy stunt anyway?"

Jordan thought about it. "Which one?"

Kowalsky's expression grew confidential. "You know which one I mean, all right. I'm talking about that first night down in my office. All that stuff about a check Kyle was supposed to have given you. Conning me to send deputies out there and all. I give you a break and what do I get, egg on my face!"

Jordan bent down, tucking a handkerchief inside the steel loop chafing his flesh. "Somebody killed her. My guess was Kyle. I thought maybe he'd panic when he saw the law on his doorstep." It was weak but he had no intention of surrendering the truth that was locked in his mind. Especially not now.

Kowalsky pondered the answer. "I'm a fair man, Brady,

whether you believe it or not. My deputies went through three checkbooks. There wasn't a single stub made out in your name. And you know something — there wasn't even one with three hundred seventy-five dollars written on it!" He jerked his head at his reflection in the mirror, pleased with his point.

The tires sang along on the softened tarmac. One of the stubs was a forgery. It had to be. Kyle had outsmarted them all. A squirrel buckjumped its way across the road. Kowalsky swerved to avoid it.

"Ever see one of them little fellers on the job, Brady?"

Jordan ignored him. "I said *somebody* killed her."

"That's right, too," Kowalsky allowed. "How'd you come to pick on Donatelli anyway?"

It was plain that whatever the verdict of the jury, the sheriff did not agree with it.

Jordan's smile was lopsided. "I had a dream."

The remark sent Kowalsky into a hostile silence. They crossed a six-lane highway and dropped down through a forest. The redwoods echoed their passing. Another quarter-hour brought them out on a plateau. A signpost directed them. SPRINGFIELD TWO MILES AHEAD. The advice was super-fluous. There was nowhere else to go. A waste of scrubland stretched to a straggling fringe of cypresses on the cliffs bordering the ocean. A double row of barbed wire hedged in a colony of single-story buildings. Guard towers stood at the corners of the complex. Kowalsky touched his horn ring. Somebody in the gatehouse tripped a switch. The barrier in the wire started to rise slowly. There was an impression of color after the neutral hues of the sun-scorched plateau. Lush

Bermuda grass was growing between the red cedar buildings. Kowalsky braked in front of the gatehouse. He heaved himself sideways, searching his pants for the handcuff key. Jordan kneaded his ankle tenderly. Kowalsky showed no sign of leaving the car. A tanned guard in a light blue uniform came out of the gatehouse.

"He's all yours," said Kowalsky. "Watch him. He's as slippery as a bullfrog."

He handed the guard the manila envelope and started his motor. Jordan took his bags from the car. The Stars and Stripes stirred on the mast overhead. It was mercifully cool inside the gatehouse. There were flowers in a vase near the phone, a wicker chair with cushions. The guard touched a switch, watching the sheriff's car through the barrier. He was a young man and friendly.

"I guess you're not carrying any guns or files, are you, mac?"

Jordan dropped his two bags on the floor. "They don't allow them in county jail."

The guard grinned back. "I'll take your word for it." He threw a pair of jeans at Jordan. "Those look like your size. If they need any altering, take them to the tailor's shop in the morning. Keep your shirt, socks, and underwear. And your shoes."

The jeans fitted well enough. The guard rummaged through the property envelope. He gave Jordan his watch and pencil. "You want these, it's at your own risk. Maybe I shouldn't say this but we've got some characters here like never seem to learn."

Jordan strapped on his watch. The guard's expression was

good humored. He pushed a mimeographed map across the table. It displayed the layout of the camp in detail. There were six bunkhouses, a dining hall, a library, and a recreation center. The various workshops were situated side by side behind a swimming pool. The guard pointed at the code key.

"Here's the camp director's office and the surgery. You see the doc first. The director will tell you where you bunk. Collect your kit from the commissary store. Any stuff you want from your bags you can pick up later." He threw the door open.

Jordan heard the barking of seals on the rocks below. The thirty-meter pool glistened invitingly.

"You mean that I walk out — just like that?" Jordan queried.

The guard's wave emphasized his point. "You can ride a bike for all I care — if you can find one. You'd better get used to it, feller. Life here's a helluva lot different from county jail. We've got pretty much the same sort of rules that they have on the street. Loaf on your work and they'll fire you. You'll probably finish up doing something a whole lot less pleasant. There's one thing you'd better remember. Those guys up on the towers are for real. They don't like you coming too close to that wire. OK?"

Jordan nodded, shielding his eyes against the bright light outside. He could see the glint of submachine guns up in the towers. He used the map to find his way past a carpenter's shop noisy with hammering, a shop with clattering power presses. A lanky gray-haired man unwound himself out of a nearby flower bed.

62

"You got the time on you, buddy?"

Jordan checked his watch. The whole thing was unreal. "Five after three."

The man groaned and spat. "*Jeeee*sus! Two more hours of it. I never lived this close to nature before. Welcome to Dotheboys Hall. The doc's office over there." He pointed and dropped like a stone on his backside.

The surgery door was open. A short man with silver hair and Japanese features was staining slides in a sink. The place was bright and spotless. A couple of hospital cots showed through an inner doorway. The Japanese spoke over his shoulder.

"Take a seat, please. I'll be right with you."

Jordan showed the pack of butts. "Is it all right to smoke?"

"Go ahead!" The Oriental rinsed his fingers under the faucet and flipped a blank card out of a drawer. "All you have to tell me is your name and age."

"Brady Jordan. I'm thirty-six."

Most of his teeth were gold. He showed them frequently. "I'm Wally Tamaru. Before you make any cracks, my family's been here for three generations. Is anything worrying you — healthwise, I mean?"

Jordan flipped the spent match through the doorway. "I never felt better in my life."

Tamaru's eyes were black beads in slits of skin. He wore issue jeans under his surgical smock.

"That's it then, Brady. You'll get all your tests tomorrow: lungs, teeth, and cardiograph. If you're sick you can see me at any time. I won't be going anywhere for the next three years seven months and two days. And don't worry about my qual-

63

ifications. I used to lecture in neurosurgery. A doctor comes in from the outside twice a week. That's to make sure I'm not killing you guys off too rapidly. The inscrutable orient, you know." He smiled again and bowed from the neck.

Jordan lifted a hand. "Thanks, Doc. Where do I go now?"

Tamaru pointed across the watered grass. "George's office. The one with the door knocker."

Jordan peered out dubiously. "The guy on the gate said I had to see the camp director."

Tamaru's expression was bland. "George *is* the camp director."

The office was like the rest of the buildings in the complex, with spacious windows set in red cedar walls. The door knocker was made in the shape of a truncated hand, the fingers pointing upward. Jordan lifted it.

A booming voice answered. "Come right in!"

Bear skins lay on the waxed polished boards. The walls were hung with washy watercolors of fishermen mending nets, dragging their boats over bleached beaches. The general air of poverty identified the locale as Mexico. All four windows in the room were open. A large man lumbered forward behind outstretched hand. A fringe of grizzled hair clung to his balding scalp. Heavy spectacles framed his earnest gaze. He was wearing a Saks safari shirt with epaulettes. A raw silk scarf was knotted on one side of his stringy neck. Bermuda shorts and *huaraches* completed his outfit. Jordan found the overall effect highly suspect but reserved judgment. Nothing he had seen so far conformed to his ideas of a penal institution. He flexed his fingers surreptitiously. The director's handshake had left them numbed. A ball game

64

was in progress on the screen of a portable television set. The sound was turned off.

The director pushed a chair at his visitor. "Sit you down, Brady."

Jordan lowered himself gingerly, his eyes on the littered table between them. He could just see the blown-up morgue shots of Joanne Kyle under a sheaf of typescript. The director's hand hovered over a cigarette box.

"I think I've got most brands — any preference?"

Jordan chose at random. The director touched the sheaf of paper. "Judge Sherman's a friend of mine. That's how your file comes to be here. They sent it over just as soon as we had the OK from the bureau that you'd be coming to us."

Jordan kept his voice civil in spite of the feeling of outrage. "I don't see how those pictures belong here. The jury acquitted me on the charge of murder."

The director's face creased with concern. "I want you to listen to me, Brady. That's the last time I want to hear the word 'murder' used around here. All this stuff on the table belongs to the past. My concern is with the future. There's only one purpose for me having that file — to help me get to know you better."

The desk sign read GEORGE FLETCHER. The ball game flickered on in the sudden silence. Fletcher broke it.

"You've been through a deeply traumatic experience, Brady. I understand far more than you may think. I've got to have your trust if I'm going to be of any use to you."

There was something disarming in the man's sincerity. Jordan spread his hands. "I was just thinking. If Sherman's a friend of yours I've got two strikes against me already. I'm not a fool. I could see what was on his mind when he sentenced me. I didn't kill that woman but the trouble is that nobody but the jury believes me. It's an odd reflection to have to carry around for the rest of your life."

"Aren't we being a mite sorry for ourselves?" Fletcher asked mildly. He selected a pipe from a rack and sucked on the empty bowl.

Jordan shrugged. "I'm not sure what I'm supposed to say to that."

The spectacles magnified the director's earnestness. "Whatever you feel like saying, Brady — within the framework of good manners. That's how we do things here. For instance, you're not supposed to call me a homosexual, not to my face, anyway. But nobody'll hit you over the head with a sap if you do. This is an experimental institution. There's no hole, no earning privileges. Everyone starts off with exactly the same rights. If a guy fouls out we try to find an appropriate punishment. The really tough cases we ship back to state prison. I understand you're a writer, Brady. What sort of stuff did you write?"

Already it was in the past tense. Jordan pointed at the table. "You'll find it there in the trial record — all of it. And in case you're going to suggest that I change my profession, that's already been done. They tell me there's a good future for a guy with a shovel."

Fletcher's pipe showered the table with fragments of smoldering tobacco. He slapped at them hastily.

"You're making me nervous, darn it. Tell me about Hollywood — the writing part I mean. All one knows is what one reads."

Jordan's smile was stony. "What's to tell — it's no different from any other place. All you need is talent, luck, and a well-honed dagger. I was what they called a troublemaker. That means I had the nerve to tell a star she had no brains."

Fletcher nodded as if he understood. "Incidentally you call me 'George.' I'd like to talk about this some more, Brady. In the meantime don't worry about Hal Sherman. I've proven him wrong before. Are you married by the way?"

Jordan had an uneasy feeling that the brown myopic eyes watching him were less naive than he supposed.

"I wanted to be," he answered. "It didn't work out."

The director clasped his hands around bony knees. "It's not as tragic as you might think — in here at least. I'm by no means a misogynist but these are facts. Of the fifty odd guys in here over half are inside because of women. I'll pass from the subject as delicately as I can. It's generally easier for an unmarried man to make parole. There are reasons that I won't bother to go into now but it's true."

"Crazy," said Jordan. He could think of nothing else.

The director switched off the television set. "I'll show you around the place. I'm putting you to work in the library. Did you ever hear of an actor called Ballantine — Scott Ballantine, a Canadian?"

Jordan dredged his memory without success. "I guess not. But that wouldn't mean a thing. Actors are even thicker on the ground than writers in Hollywood. Should I have?"

Fletcher rubbed his scalp, blinking. "I'm not entirely sure. Probably not. The thing is that you'll be working with him. You'll find you have a lot in common."

Jordan leaned over the desk and stubbed out his butt.

67

"Fair enough. I'm not making any secret of it; I want out of here as soon as I can. I'll work with anyone."

The director raised a monitory finger. "I'd better warn you, don't get dazzled by Scott's dialogue. You'll hear it all — that there's no place for the concept of justice in modern penology and so on. Scott has a good mind but it's biased. He has a healthily cynical regard for us all and basically he's a nice guy. You'll be talking the same language. It should help."

Jordan followed the director through the door. "Shouldn't I ask what he's in for?"

The director dropped a straw hat squarely on his head. They started across grass that was still wet from the water sprinklers.

"He'll tell you himself. He's serving his maximum sentence. He lost every day of his good time up at state prison. They sent him to us as incorrigible."

They passed the bent, resentful figure weeding the flower bed. The director waved. The man straightened his back. His assumed falsetto voice was just short of insulting. Fletcher chuckled.

"That's a sample of our system at work. Harry's still sore. He's got two more days of it. He stole somebody's shirt in the bunkhouse. It didn't even fit him. He liked the color, he said. We've asked him to wear it for a week."

The library doors were open and protected with fly netting. It was ten degrees cooler inside. The walls were lined with bookshelves. Racks of periodicals stood beside the reading tables. A six-footer with fairish hair curling over his collar came across the room to meet them. Jordan's first impression was one of elegance. The man's jeans had been pounded to the texture of linen. His wing-tip shoes were old but highly polished. His shirt was spotless. He looked at the director with wary blue eyes.

Fletcher wrapped an arm around Jordan's shoulders. "This is Brady Jordan, Scott. The chap I was telling you about."

Ballantine had the mobile mouth of an actor and a nose that had been broken at one time. He jerked his thumb at the table where he had been sitting. A newspaper was spread out on it.

"Hi! I've been following your exploits avidly. Fascinating. Allow me to offer my hearty congratulations." His grin showed good teeth. He seemed to be mocking himself rather than Jordan.

Fletcher removed his arm. "He'll bunk with you, Scott. It'll make things easier all around. You'll be able to show him the ropes."

"Will do," the Canadian said easily. "Was there anything else, George?"

The director blinked hard. "There was, as a matter of fact. Tamaru's supply of alcohol has vanished yet again. Naturally he knows nothing. The empty bottle was found in back of the tennis court. I thought you might have seen it there. I understand you were playing after breakfast."

Ballantine crossed his heart solemnly. "You know me better than that, George. I've always refused to be a party to that sort of low intrigue."

The director's gaze took in the room. "Just an academic observation, Scott. Nothing more. But we're spiking the

69

stuff from now on. You might see that the word gets around."

He exited on the line, smiling at them both in turn as he went through the door. Ballantine watched him cut across the grass. Jordan could see the headline on the newspaper he had been reading. The date was yesterday's.

END NEAR IN KYLE SLAYING

The Canadian swung around. "God's good. George loves you."

He fished behind a row of books and came up with a bottle. Another shelf produced a thermos full of ice cubes. He made a couple of drinks and poured them into paper cups. He gave one to Jordan.

"Drink hearty — it's the last of a vintage year. May your superlative luck continue to flourish."

Jordan choked on the fiery mixture. Orange juice barely disguised the bite of hospital alcohol. When they were done, Ballantine put a match to the paper cups and rinsed the thermos in the bathroom. When he came out again he was smiling.

"Don't think we fooled George. But then he loves me, too. I guess I'd better make that clear. My position here is a privileged one. I can belch in chapel, pick flowers — raise hell in general. I achieved the distinction the hard way. I don't *have* any more good time for them to take away. And it's too much trouble for them to send me back to state prison. George wouldn't go for it, anyway."

Jordan had a strange feeling that he had come home. "I heard. I was told to be careful of your dialectics. Tell me something — is George to be taken seriously?"

Ballantine forked a chair. His open shirt showed a lean tanned body.

"You mean the fag or the missionary? Don't let George fool you with either production. There's a big brain beating under that bald dome. And he's got a hound dog's nose for anything that's not strictly kosher. Have you thought about parole yet — sure you have — I mean the date?"

The date was firmly etched in Jordan's mind. "Someone told me June."

Ballantine was fingering one of his long sideburns. "June's right. It's the same month that I hit the street. I've been here nearly two years. I've watched them come and go. Do you know how many men make parole at the first hearing? One in five!"

"You're kidding!" Jordan's voice was shocked.

The Canadian nodded. "A list goes up once a month in the Recreation Room. I'm the guy who types it. A list of men due to make their first parole applications. You'll see them, reading their names, the think balloons coming out of their ears. They're all so sure they've got the thing licked. They've either made or promised restitution — the board's high on that. Some minister of the gospel has been coerced into backing the application. The little woman's written in saying that she's waiting there with open arms. And what happens — they stagger out of the boardroom wondering what hit them. 'Come back and see us in a year's time,' says Brannigan. He's the chairman of the board and he dotes on George. In fact, we all dote on George around here. You'll find that it pays."

"You mean George is the express line to parole?"

"The only one," said the Canadian. He pulled a drawer in

71

the table and produced a typewritten sheet. He offered it for Jordan's inspection, his face now serious. "Take a look at this. It's a copy of what you'll have to sign before you're paroled."

Jordan read the sheet through with growing disbelief.

Conditions of Parole

1) I shall proceed directly to my place of parole and make my report within twenty-four hours. I shall have in my possession all money given to me at my release except for a necessary expenditure for travel, food, and shelter.

2) I will not leave the state or community without the written permission of my parole officer.

3) I will conduct myself as a good citizen. I understand that this means that I may not associate with evil companions or individuals having criminal records. I must avoid questionable resorts, abstain from wrongdoing, lead an honest, upright, and industrious life, support my dependents, if any, and assume toward them all my moral and legal obligations. My behavior must not be a menace to the safety of my family, or to any individual or group of individuals.

4) I will carry out the instructions of my parole officer, allow him to visit me at my residence and place of employment. I will not change my employment or residence without first obtaining the permission of my parole officer. If I lose my job for any reason I will report this to my parole officer immediately. I will cooperate with him in his efforts to obtain for me gainful employment.

5) I may be required to be in my home at an hour at night determined by my parole officer.

6) I will not indulge in the use of or sale of narcotics and will abstain from the use of intoxicating liquor.

7) I will not marry without consulting and obtaining the written permission of my parole officer nor will I live with as man and wife or have sex relations with any woman not my lawful wife.

8) I will surrender to my parole officer immediately after my release any motor vehicle license I may have had in my possession at the time of my arrest. I will not make application for a motor vehicle license or for any license permitting me to carry firearms of any nature without permission of the parole officer.

9) I may not work in any place where liquor is sold or made without the written permission of the state liquor authority authorizing such employment.

10) If I should be arrested in another state during the period of my parole I will waive extradition and will not resist being returned to the Board of Parole of this state.

11) I will report to my parole officer each and every time that I am arrested or questioned by any law enforcement agency and will give all the facts and circumstances that brought about such arrest or questioning.

12) I hereby certify that I have read and understood the foregoing conditions of my parole.

Signed ———

Jordan looked up incredulously. The other man's smile was sardonic. "I thought the style would appeal to you. They waive the second half of number eight in time of war."

The ground was slipping from under Jordan's feet. "I don't believe it," he said. "The whole thing's archaic."

Ballantine tossed the paper back in the drawer. "Let me tell you what you're thinking. You're thinking that I can't make parole so I knock the system. That it's a case of sour grapes. Well you're wrong. Only one man in five gets to live that honest upright life at his first appearance and this is why. It's something that very few of them latch onto. The moment George gives you the handshake he typecasts you. He never alters his opinion. Be whatever he wants you to be and you're in. George knows your role — the trick is to discover it yourself. It's difficult but not impossible."

The waning match burned Jordan's fingers. He lit another and dragged smoke into his lungs.

"I've got to get out of here as soon as I can. If it's help I need, I'm willing to pay for the ride."

Ballantine cocked his head. "Are you, now?"

"Cash," said Jordan.

"That's a rich-sounding word — cash!" The Canadian seemed to watch it curl away in the air. Then he was serious. "I just might take a chance on you. What have I got to lose? After nearly six years of it I'm 'hostile to authority,' as they say."

Seventy-two months. Five mountains to climb wearily before you slid down the far side of the year. The thought was frightening. "I don't know how you've done it," Jordan said sincerely. "I couldn't."

"You'd do your best," Ballantine said lightly. "A day at a time. There's no other way, short of taking a rope. Let's not get morbid. Let's talk about George. It's more important. He knows that I lifted that alcohol the same way that he knows that I've used his phone a couple of times. I've never broken the rules of our own private game — it's different now. I'm on to George, Brady. He's God in a bush shirt. And I'm an atheist. I don't want your money. I want to beat this parole system. I can't do it myself but I can do it through you. You're made to order for me. I'll show you where you sleep."

He led the way across the grass to a nearby building. The interior of the bunkhouse was cheerful with travel posters. Two rows of beds stood against the walls, four beds to a row. Photographs and calendars decorated the metal lockers between them. Ballantine pushed a door, displaying the wash basins, toilets, and shower stalls.

"The water's always hot," he informed. "We take it in turns to clean the place up. That is, you guys do. I'm exempt. Favoritism. This is your bed."

He bounced a mattress with his foot. Sheets and blankets were like army issue but clean. A salt breeze was blowing through the open windows. Barbed wire was strung between the cypresses along the cliff. A couple hundred yards away the long swell of the Pacific broke against the rocky shores of the seal colony. Ballantine perched on the bed opposite.

"It's a whole lot easier on the eye than state prison. Think about my proposition, Brady. There are no strings attached, but you'll have to play it my way."

Jordan stuffed his spare jeans into his locker. "I'll think about it."

Ballantine stretched out and put a pillow under his head. "I'm psychic. Give me a week and I'll tell you what part George has given you in his soap opera."

Jordan rinsed his mouth in the bathroom annex. A soap scrawl across the mirror said:

> *Don't you guys want to see your ugly faces?*
> *Get this mirror cleaned!*

It was the first time in weeks that he'd seen himself in a good light. The badger streak of white in his hair seemed to have grown wider. His skin was sun starved. He came back smiling.

"I've written this kind of dialogue. This is the moment when I ask you what you're in for."

Ballantine aimed his words at the ceiling. "I tried, God knows I tried!"

Jordan suspected that the sarcasm might hide real feeling. It would probably be self-pity. All actors were alike.

"If you're touchy about it, forget it," he said amiably.

Ballantine lifted his head. "Who's touchy! On the contrary, it's very important to establish the correct pecking order. The Mafiosi and con men are at the top — sexual deviates at the bottom. We don't have any Mafiosi here. Come to think of it, you rank pretty low yourself. This pot thing's a meatball rap."

Jordan laughed in spite of himself. "Where do you come in?"

Ballantine sat up straight again. "A little bit higher but not much. Everything I did stinks of the amateur. That has to be taken into consideration. Here I was sitting in a bar on the Strip, trying to think how I could keep my car from being repossessed. You know the score — an actor's as successful as his appearance. A bunch of sports picked me up and took me to this party in the hills. Surrounded by all that unfamiliar luxury, the training of a God-fearing Ontario home went for nothing. In short I clipped my hostess's jewelry. The law busted me the next day in Vegas, trying to fence the loot."

76

The banality of the account disappointed Jordan. "Was this your first exercise in larceny?"

Ballantine waved a lazy hand. "The first off screen. It seems to be tougher in practice. The cops are too well informed. The judge called it a 'deliberate and blatant betrayal of hospitality.' He gave me five-to-six. George thinks I was harshly treated. That's one of the reasons why he loves me. Let's get back to the library."

Jordan lowered his legs. It was beginning to look as if the Fate Sisters had finally remembered him.

The nights became colder, the sunshine a little paler. The first three months were tough ones for Jordan. The days were no problem. He read a great deal and talked with Ballantine. The library was used infrequently. Most of the cons spent their free time watching television in the Recreation Room. He made no friends apart from Ballantine. They ate together, walked together, constantly exploring one another's intelligence. The pact between them had long since been established. Masterminding Jordan's parole was to be the Canadian's final gesture — the last snook cocked at a system he despised.

Jordan was an apt pupil. The camp director watched their association like a broody hen. He took to dropping in for coffee with them in the library. They'd sit there chatting. Ballantine's role was the hard-nosed cynic. George took the Canadian's jibes with good humor. The director's eyes were always on Jordan, as if waiting for some expected revelation. Jordan leaked it gradually — an almost reluctant acceptance of the director's values. The three soon became a twosome, Ballantine excusing himself. Now it was George who talked, earnestly and at length.

". . . you've heard Scott say it — there isn't a single crime in the penal code that hasn't been held to be a civic virtue, someplace, sometime. It's true but this is an observation not an argument. Laws are a matter of expediency, no matter how we try to dignify them with moral values. This we simply have to accept, Brady. I'm concerned with present realities. We're living in the twentieth century but I'm dead sure of one thing. To survive we've got to love one another. And I don't mean L-O-V-E. Laugh if you like."

It was the last thing Jordan had in mind. He looked as if he'd heard revealed truth. It was two days afterward that Ballantine told him that they had it made.

December ended with apple pie and ice cream. Each inmate was issued one bottle of beer. Television viewing privileges were extended till one A.M. The entire camp herded into the Recreation Room, watching the West Coast herald in the new year.

Jordan lay awake long after the bunkhouse was quiet, seeing Joanne's face. Freedom was no more than the means to avenge her. His plan had taken shape over the months. Now he needed help to get it off the ground. He heard a movement from the bed opposite and propped himself up. A searchlight beam swept through the bunkhouse. The Canadian was awake.

"Can't you sleep either?" Jordan asked quietly.

"Just thinking." The Canadian sounded tired.

Jordan peered across the room. "I want to talk to you in the morning. It could be important for both of us." There was a strange sense of relief in going even this far.

Ballantine's face showed in the match flame. "I've been waiting for that. Sleep well."

They were alone in the library. It was past eleven. George had come and gone. Jordan locked both doors.

"Last night you said you'd been waiting — waiting for what?"

Ballantine tipped back his chair and put his legs on his desk. "That really got to you, didn't it? You're going to talk to me about Kyle."

Jordan looked at him steadily. A couple of inches of hair hung raggedly over the Canadian's collar. He used a razor and a couple of mirrors to cut it himself.

"That's right," said Jordan. "It works out now that if I make parole I hit the street two days after you do."

Ballantine's voice was casual. "You'll make parole all right. I peeked in George's desk last night. Your recommendation's in there, already written. I'll give you a quote. 'This inmate has shown a sense of adjustment and an acceptance of responsibility that may well have been an example to others.' 'Others,' I assume, means me. All you have to do now is keep the wheels oiled and turning."

The news brought a surge of excitement. "You've done a lot for me, Scott," said Jordan. "It's time for me to do something for you. How would you like five thousand dollars?"

Ballantine lowered his feet to the ground. "That sounds like an awful lot of money. What do I have to do for it?"

Jordan made his voice emphatic. "Help me settle a contract. I'm not asking you to do anything that's illegal. All I want you to do is get a piece of paper for me."

"The check," said Ballantine. He held a hand up. "Look, Brady, it's simple enough. I've listened to your story twenty times or more. I've read through your trial record — every newspaper report — it has to be the check."

Jordan relaxed. Ballantine was telling the truth. He'd been a sounding board over the past months. Time and again they had gone through the evidence together. The only thing he had withheld was his own will for revenge. Now even that didn't matter. All he had to do was frame it in such a way that the other man would accept.

"There'll be no danger," he promised. "I've a good idea where the check is hidden. You're going to walk into the Kyle house as a guest. I'll show you how."

Ballantine's eyes crinkled. "Nothing illegal, no danger, and five thousand dollars. Why don't you do it yourself?"

It was an obvious question and Jordan had the answer. "How many reasons would you like? I can think of four offhand."

"They'll keep," said Ballantine. "Tell me something else first. Who do *you* think killed your girl?"

Jordan shrugged. "Your guess is as good as mine. But the check will help me find out."

"And then?"

It was the question he feared. "Nothing's going to bring her back. But I *can* make Kyle pay for what he's done to me."

Ballantine switched the subject. "You know, I've got a

theory that innocence is its own defense. I've seen it work. Even in your case it worked."

Jordan laughed outright. "This is something I never thought I'd hear you say. I think you're a phony, Scott. I wouldn't be surprised if you told me you believed in Santa Claus. You know as well as I do that a smart lawyer beat that rap for me. Without him I'd have finished in the gas chamber."

Ballantine's face was obstinate. "He worked with what he had — the knowledge that you were innocent. Who cares, anyway? It's no more than a point of view. You know something — I do believe in Santa Claus. Tell me how he's going to get me into the Kyle house."

Jordan was silent for a moment. He looked at the other, level eyed.

"Remember that nobody's twisting your arm. Say the word and we'll forget the whole thing. But if you *are* in, it'll be me who calls the plays. It'll be your turn to do what you're told. Can you *do* what you're told, Scott?"

Ballantine's answer was to go next door into the annex. He reappeared carrying a couple of paper cups.

"I held out on you," he grinned. "It wasn't quite the last. I was saving this for a celebration. No danger, no illegality, and five thousand bucks. *Salut!*"

Jordan downed the raw spirit. Ballantine's trouble was that he never stopped acting. The obsession cut both ways and would have to be watched.

"*Salut!*" he replied.

Scott Ballantine   June 1970

THEY WERE LYING on the grass under the vast oak behind the commissary. The carved initials of successful parolees scarred the bark. It was almost six o'clock. The glass walls of the machine-gun towers flashed in the evening sunshine. He heard the shout as the relief guard climbed the ladder to the platform. Ballantine shifted his head. Jordan was on his back, chewing a blade of grass, eyes shut. Nine months had changed his appearance. The exposed parts of his skin were only a shade lighter than the tan shirt he was wearing. Fat no longer blurred his jawline. Fresh air and exercise had honed his body. Ballantine used a foot to prod his comrade into consciousness.

"Take a look at what's coming."

Jordan shaded one eye, inspecting the figure swaying toward them.

"Someone at the agency's on the ball," he said, and closed his eyes again.

General Jordan, Ballantine thought with a moment's sourness. One swift glance fixes the enemy positions in the keen soldierly mind. Blow taps and sleep soundly, men. The general's watching over you. Jordan's new confidence dated from the moment he'd officially known that he'd made parole. It irritated Ballantine that his own part in the production seemed to have been forgotten.

The man coming toward them was walking as if his knees were held together by an elastic band. Short tripping steps accentuated the swing of his buttocks. He was wearing a white nylon shirt with a large monogram worked on the breast pocket. The general impression of genteel effeminacy was marred by a voice like a bosun's.

"Ah've been lookin' all ovah for you-all," he complained.

Ballantine rose on his elbows, imitating the thick hominy-grits accent. "Well ah declaiuh!"

The newcomer was the camp director's orderly. It was a new post, especially created for him. He took it seriously. He looked from one to the other accusingly. "Hidin' away! What you-all find to talk about ah cain't imagine!"

Jordan came to life suddenly. "That's because you haven't been exposed to a classical education. Beat it!"

The orderly stood his ground. "Drug fiend!" he said scathingly. "George wants you now, heah, Ballantine?" He flounced away.

Ballantine hauled himself up. "Graduation Day."

"You're going out in the world, my boy," Jordan intoned. "There'll be pitfalls and temptations."

Ballantine brushed the grass from his pants. "And you're a lot less humorous than you think, most of the time."

Jordan squinted up. "I do my best. Watch it with George, that's all. I'll wait here."

Ballantine nodded. A group of swimmers had waylaid the orderly, threatening to throw him into the pool. He fended them off, limp armed, squealing with delight. Ballantine's bunkhouse was empty. He looked around it for the last time. The routine of release was familiar to him. He must have seen a couple hundred men make the same trip. First came the session with George, the last handshakes, then the walk to the Liberty Rooms attached to the gatehouse. Men due for release slept there on the last night. Six years to the day, he thought suddenly. No night without some memory of the past. No day without thought of the future.

He collected a few things from his locker. There were no letters for him to keep or destroy. The last piece of mail he'd received had been four weeks after his conviction. The card was from a cousin in Saskatoon suggesting that prayer was a panacea for everything. He made a pile of his unwanted clothes and left them on his bed. The bag at the gate held everything he needed. He walked across to George's office. The windows were wide open. Ballantine pushed the door. The room smelled of George's cologne — a manly tangy scent to tone with the bear rugs on the floor. The camp director blinked welcome. His bush shirt was freshly ironed, his Bermuda shorts of a gay plaid pattern.

"Well, Scott. The big moment at last — how does it feel?"

Ballantine switched a chair under his rear. George seemed to think that freedom was his personal invention.

"Weird," Ballantine said shortly. "It's been a long time." He took a cigarette from the choice on the table. He managed to keep his eyes from the bound manuscript on the blotter. A label was pasted on the cover:

FROM THE INSIDE OUT

A Fictitious Case History

by
Brady Jordan

85

Ballantine leaned into the flame that George was offering. Jordan's piece would never earn a nickel but it had achieved its purpose. Researched in depth, it portrayed the healing of a troubled mind by a skilled and dedicated counselor. It was a clever piece of propaganda just short of downright flattery. The camp director had had it Xeroxed and circulated among his friends.

"Not feeling scared?" George asked suddenly.

Ballantine's eyes widened. "What would I be scared of?"

George nibbled a cuticle, sneaking a look at the papers on his blotter. "I usually give a quick shuffle through the uglier facts of life on the outside, finishing with the bit about making a friend of your parole officer. That doesn't apply to you. In fact, I'm not sure what I'm supposed to say to you, Scott. Your friend's an entirely different problem."

Ballantine trapped the ball and returned it neatly. "Which friend would that be?"

George smiled wisely. "Oh, come on, Scott. We know one another better than that. I'm talking about Brady Jordan. I'll be frank with you. It's Brady I'm concerned with, not you. You've been pretty close to him. That's why I'm talking like this."

Ballantine shrugged. "He's your problem not mine."

The camp director seemed to sag a little. "Strange. I'd have thought that a friendship forged in jail would mean more than that."

Ballantine's eyebrows rose. "What is this, George? You put Brady to work with me — great. It made things easier for both of us. But I'm *leaving* here tomorrow. Once I'm through that gate, I can't hold his hand anymore."

George wiped the lens of his spectacles with the corner of a silk handkerchief. His eyes were myopic.

"You mean you won't be seeing him on the outside?"

The Canadian thumbed his butt into the ashtray. You've *got* to be joking! He's paroled to his aunt, isn't he? You know the rules — he can't afford to be seen with an ex-con. I've got troubles of my own, anyway."

George brooded on the thought. Suddenly he tapped the paper in front of him. "I'm going to stick my neck out and tell you what's in this bit of light literature. It's a confidential report on the Kyle case from the office of the Fairfax County Prosecutor — a Mr. Abbott. It seems that Kyle's worried by the news of Jordan's parole. Worried enough to ask for police protection."

Ballantine opened his mouth wide and laughed. "That's really something. All the time we've been together I've never heard Brady mention Kyle once. It's not his bag anymore, believe me, George."

The director sounded doubtful. "I hope so. A copy of this report has gone to the bureau. They're going to be breathing down Brady's neck. The first wrong move he makes he'll be back inside. I want him to be very sure of that. I thought he might take the news better from you than from me."

Ballantine stretched out his legs, looking at his shoes. "It sounds as if this Kyle had a guilty conscience or something. Did he get his protection?"

George locked the file in a drawer. "No, he didn't. They tell me that some maniac is starting fires all over Fairfax County. The Sheriff Department has other things to do. You'll see Brady before you go to the gatehouse, of course."

87

It was a statement rather than a question. Ballantine rose, fingering the scar where the flying puck had broken his nose.

"You want me to tell him about Kyle. OK. Nothing else?"

George looked like a sheep dog that is losing one of its flock.

"I guess not, Scott. It's been good knowing you. None of the noises I can make will alter any decisions you've made. I can only wish you luck."

Ballantine retrieved his fingers. Bad breath and all, the guy was sincere. "Thanks for everything, George."

The director hesitated. "If you're ever in a jam — I mean for cash . . ."

"I'll call you, reverse charges." Ballantine picked up the plastic bag. It contained his toothbrush and a piece of soap. There was no need for either of them to believe what he had said. The gesture had been made.

Outside mist creeping in from the ocean partially hid the sun. The seal rookery was already obscured. He quickened his step, sensing that George was watching from the window. He half turned, lifting a hand in salute. He had no regrets — not even about engineering Jordan's parole. Ice cream and pie, prerelease movies, wearing your own shoes — none of it altered the fact that Springfield was a penal institution. The machine-gun towers would still cut loose at a guy making a dash for freedom. You played according to their rules and did the best you could for yourself meanwhile. No one had the right to say that he hadn't given George good value.

He passed various groups of men, indifferent to the occasional shout of farewell. They were few enough. He'd courted unpopularity. "The loneliness of the elite" his father had called it. The remark had baffled Ballantine at the time. It had been difficult to conceive an elite of elderly fruit farmers sitting around talking about the Jacobite succession. Maybe what his father had really meant was the loneliness of the rebel. That much Ballantine understood.

Jordan was still on his back under the oak tree. He rose on an elbow as Ballantine squatted beside him.

"Well?"

The Canadian dragged a piece of grass out by the roots. "We talked about you. Kyle's asked for police protection."

Jordan's green eyes darkened. The news seemed to disturb him. "Did he get it?"

Ballantine threw the grass away. "No. There's a firebug loose in the county. George is worried that you might do something foolish. It got me worrying, too."

Jordan spread the corners of his mouth. "See what I mean — no faith. I hope you put him straight."

Ballantine leaned back on his palms. "I was thinking about something, walking over from George's office. State prison provided me with another education. The routines I learned. I ought to be the best all-round man in the larceny business. But something's missing." He tapped himself in the region of his heart.

Jordan's manner changed noticeably. "I thought we'd laid that ghost to rest for once and for all."

"So did I," Ballantine said quietly.

Jordan rested his chin on his knees. "Don't tell me you want out now!"

Ballantine shook his head. "I didn't say that either. You've promised me five grand to bring you that check. I need five grand for the *dolce vita*. I may be the year's prize sucker but I trust you. It's just the mechanics of the thing that makes me nervous."

Jordan came a little closer. "I'm not asking you to break into Fort Knox. How many times have we been into this already, for crissakes! You're going to look for a loose floorboard in a house where you're a guest. There's no law against it."

Ballantine recognized the doubt in his voice. "It's the loose floorboard that worries me."

The green eyes watching him were steady. "You don't believe me?"

"I believe you," answered Ballantine hastily. "I have to."

Ninety-nine times out of a hundred he did. It was the odd one that bugged him. He'd studied Jordan's trial record and reread the newspaper clippings. A wave of arbitrary arrests had followed the acquittal. A succession of bums and drifters, sexual deviates from half a dozen cities, had been picked up. A baker in San Diego had confessed to Joanne Kyle's murder. Investigation showed him to be kneading a cupcake mix two hundred miles away at the time of the crime. The Kyle case had collapsed into a bundle of papers at the bottom of a drawer somewhere in the county prosecutor's office. It seemed that as far as all were concerned they could stay there. Yet Joanne Kyle certainly hadn't strangled herself. Nor had Jordan. That much Ballantine did believe.

He checked his watch. "I'm due at the gatehouse."

"You still haven't answered me," Jordan pointed out.

A bell rang near the swimming pool. It was the first call for the dining hall. The air tasted of salt. Fingers of night mist were creeping over the tops of the cliffs.

"I can't afford any slip-ups," said Ballantine.

Jordan's face was exasperated. He knuckled through his short streaked hair.

"Do you think you've gotten a copyright on the idea? I stood trial for murder, remember. I've had to wonder how the first whiff of gas would taste in my mouth. Kyle made a contract with me and welshed on it. Now I want the money for my hire. The only reason you're along is because I need you to get it. Apart from that you're just another bum from Central Casting as far as I'm concerned."

It was dangerously near society's final assessment of Scott Ballantine. He buttoned his shirt. The sun was totally obscured now.

"You've made your point. It'll be noon by the time I reach Palamos. You want me to go straight to your aunt's, right?"

Jordan nodded. "Don't think you're going to be popular with her. None of my friends are. The point is that she's agreed to give you the money. Stick it out that I owe it to you. You can buy a cheap car in town as I said. You'll find some lots near the bus terminal. Then you drive back north. You know where to go — the agency in Pacific Ramparts."

The bell rang again. The line of men outside the dining hall started moving forward. They both came to their feet.

"I'll call you on Friday at your aunt's," said Ballantine. He stuck out his hand.

Jordan took it. "I'll see you, Scott. The bit about Central Casting — I didn't mean it."

There were times when Ballantine's nose ached. This was one of them. "Relax," he said, "and don't worry about a thing."

He walked toward the gatehouse wondering what he was trying to prove. He stripped for the last search. The guard's concern was that no state property should be removed, no written messages taken out. Releases from Springfield were spaced so that no more than one man left at a time. The guard gave him a clean cotton robe and let him into the Liberty Rooms. An interior decorator from Sausalito had pondered the problem of a man's final night in jail. The result was a tall-ceilinged bedroom with a view of the ocean. The bathroom was corn yellow and there was a dining area where Ballantine's food waited in a hot plate. Nothing had been forgotten. The furniture was from the Design Center in Carmel. The overall effect tended to leave the parting guests bewildered. A good percentage of their number was destined to occupy cubicles in Tolly's Temperance Taverns. Others identified home with a bug-ridden room in a Watts walk-up. There was a leather-bound book on the bedside table. George's valedictory message was typed on a slip inside the cover.

THE BIG ADVENTURE BEGINS! It's my sincere hope that our relationship has helped to fit you for it. I'd be interested in your comments on this. Say whatever you like. We too seldom know what the other guy is really thinking. Good luck!

Ballantine turned the pages. Most of the comments were tedious with flowery gratitude, pious promises for the future. A few hard-core cynics had penned their disapproval.

What Springfield needs is a good whorehouse!

Sing no sad songs for *my* soul's repose, George!
This time tomorrow I'll be thumbing my nose, George.

All time fetch and carry old bleached bones. No place here for sad African.

The last remark baffled Ballantine with its obscurity. He had no intention of adding his own views. The bag at the end of the bed held what was left of a once liberal wardrobe. There was a soft tweed jacket and a pair of fawn slacks, a drip-dry shirt of gray material. The wide cut of the trousers was an indication of their age. His identification was in an envelope: birth certificate, operator's license, citizenship papers. He'd been lucky on that score. If his conviction had come just a few months earlier he'd have been deported.

He counted the flimsy sheaf of bills that had been left there for him. One hundred and seventy dollars. After six years. What the man said was right: never take drinks from a stranger — not even Beverly Hills strangers. The dividing door between the Liberty Rooms and the gatehouse was kept locked. The dinky little phone on the table would ring at seven o'clock in the morning. Moriarty — or whoever was on duty — would announce breakfast and impending departure. The camp station wagon left for the railroad station early. It collected mail and supplies in town. Released prisoners had the ride for free.

The food in the hot plates was plentiful. He had chosen the meal himself — a parting privilege. Chicken cacciatore followed by a fresh fruit salad. Some clown in the kitchen had scrawled a farewell message on the milk container: *Eat up good — the next is gonna cost you money!*

He ate, a copy of the *National Geographic Magazine* spread in front of him. "Istanbul," he read, "the gateway to the East." "Visit Eire where cheese and whisky mature to the sound of harps." He wondered about that briefly, picturing a baronial hall lined with cheese and whisky barrels, decently draped colleens plunking their harps to the approval of the Irish Tourist Board. He washed his supper things and took a bath. He was strung up tight and swallowed a couple of the pills Tamaru had given him. The Japanese had guaranteed their effect. Twenty minutes, he said. Ballantine cut the light and stretched out on the bed. The first thing he noticed was a sensation of weightlessness. His body seemed to be shrinking till it became no more than a point of light fixed in his brain. Images passed in front of it slowly. First Jordan, the words on his moving lips soundless. Then came a large man on the order of the late Sydney Greenstreet — a composite of everything he'd heard or read about Sebastian Kyle. This voice was audible, the accent suavely British.

"So we meet at last, Mr. Ballantine!"

He opened his eyes with a start. For crissakes, he thought ruefully. This was Limehouse Nights and he was trapped in a slowly flooding cellar by the ineffable Doctor Fu Man-chu. Five seconds later he was asleep.

He beat the morning call by half an hour. The guard opened the door, bringing in coffee and food. Ballantine drank the coffee hastily. The pickup truck was waiting outside, a civilian maintenance man at the wheel. The guard was watching Ballantine reflectively. He was a lopsided bachelor who had been transferred from state prison on medical grounds. Any thoughts he had about the purpose of punishment had been formed in other circumstances. The lack of discipline at Springfield disturbed him deeply. His struggle to conform to the director's ideas resulted in frequent visits to Dave's Hideaway, the local mecca for the troubled in spirit.

"Any time *you're* ready," he said finally.

Ballantine nodded. The guy looked as if he hated to lose one from the roll call. The Canadian carried his bag out to the waiting vehicle. The driver greeted him as if the gesture hurt his head. The barrier rose and he let the pickup roll forward. Ballantine turned to take one last look at the complex of buildings. Mist wreathed the bunkhouse roofs, the television antennas glistening in the sunlight. Another forty-eight hours and Jordan would be making the same trip. *Free,* he thought suddenly. And the word really meant something. There was no more wire — no more locked doors — most important of all, no parole. The hard way had finally paid off. His suit felt good on his back, the trousers oddly light after years of wearing jeans.

The man sitting next to him was mercifully taciturn. Ballantine stared through the truck window, recognizing forgotten landmarks. The forest was in deep shadow, its still depths unpierced as yet by the early sun. The driver pulled onto the coastal highway and wheeled north for eighteen miles. The small town was strung out on both sides of the railroad tracks. Ballantine found himself looking at the most banal things with a sense of excitement — a fat boy with freckles pitching newspapers at porch fronts, a milk wagon with chimes, the bare arms of the girls waiting at the bus stops. All the women were completely desirable. He knew that it would change but right now there was nothing and no one ugly.

The driver braked the wagon to a halt in front of the depot. "There she is. You travelin' north or south?"

"South." Ballantine already had the door open. The air was heady with sweet smell from the silos across the tracks. The man showed a collection of broken teeth. "This side. She's due in two minutes after the hour. Remember me to all them wild wild wimmen."

The waiting room was empty. A few people were sitting on a bench outside the Western Union office. He walked in the opposite direction. The round-faced clock showed almost eight o'clock. A cop detached himself from an angle in the wall. He planted himself squarely in Ballantine's path, looking the Canadian over.

"Your name Ballantine, feller?"

Ballantine put down his bag. "That's right."

The cop's manner had an impatient contempt about it. "You just got out of Springfield?"

"That's right," repeated Ballantine. "What about it?" he added.

The cop was in his early thirties with narrow eyes set in a thin hard face.

"I'll ask the questions, mister. Where you heading for — got your parole papers with you?"

Ballantine felt as if he'd been readying himself for this sort of question for years. "I'm not *on* parole. I'm taking the next train south — that's unless you have any objection."

The cop's face grew happier. "Now what have we got ourselves here — a genuine little number! I'm *putting* you on that train, buster. How'd you like that?"

Ballantine's mouth had gone white at the corners. "I *don't* like it. People are watching the scene you're staging. You're subjecting me to hardship and humiliation. A smart lawyer just might be able to make something of it."

The cop hooked his thumbs in his belt but the rails started humming as he framed his answer. The arrival of the train left him wordless. Ballantine swung aboard, heaving his bag in front of him. The cop's snarl followed him.

"Hit this town again and I'll haul your ass in and give you a haircut!"

Ballantine dropped into a window seat. The day coach was almost empty. The scene with the cop had left him shaken. He was no more than an hour out of jail and bandying words with a hick policeman. He'd have to discipline his tongue somehow. Jordan's scheme required a certain amount of hard-nosed effrontery but no trouble with the law. The coach emptied and filled many times on the three-hour trip south; it was after eleven when the conductor walked through calling the next stop.

"Palamos! This stop is Palamos!"

Ballantine climbed down, squinting into the bright light. He took his bag to a seat and watched the back end of the train grow small. The shady station was quiet and deserted. He could see the usual cop out front, leaning against the side of a school bus, talking to the driver. A stubble-haired youngster was stretched out on a nearby bench, his head on a knapsack. A maple leaf emblem was stitched to the bag. His clothes looked as if he had slept in them for a week. The kid would be a fruit picker, working his way down the coast with the seasonal crops. Ballantine recalled his own arrival from Canada, fourteen years before. He'd been fresh out of drama school and certain of success. His plan of campaign had been based on Hollywood folklore. He'd play a couple of seasons in stock and the scouts would come running, brandishing checkbooks. He brought a letter of introduction with him from the principal of the drama school — a one-time character actor who had played with Barrymore. The letter produced an invitation to dinner and Ballantine's first experience of the homosexual pass. He experienced many more over the next few months. During that time he decked more people than the average prize fighter — an assembly of casting directors and booking agents, all of them anxious to befriend him. The word went around that Ballantine was a brawler and troublemaker.

He was still a Canadian citizen when war broke out in Korea and ineligible for the draft. There was work around the studios for anyone under seventy, even graduates of drama school. He learned how to have himself paged in hotel lobbies, the uselessness of squiring undistinguished starlets to Hollywood premières. Most useful of all, he learned how to block the pass sinister without breaking the protagonist's jaw. The end of the war saw him back making ads for soap operas. Hollywood never heard of him. He never got to have his nose fixed.

He pitched the spent cigarette at the railroad tracks and checked his bag. When he reached the street the cop had drifted away. He crossed to the corner drugstore and ordered the first thing he saw on the menu. There was a phone booth immediately behind him. He stepped in and fed some coins into the box. He already knew what was going to happen. He still dialed the L.A. number. A mint-fresh voice answered.

"The David Zahl Agency. Good morning!"

He gave the name of an advertising agency he had done work for years before. "We're trying to locate an actor you handle. A guy called Scott Ballantine."

"One moment please, sir." He heard her muffled aside into the intercom. Then she was back again. "Go ahead, please, you're on to Mr. David Zahl himself."

The remembered voice had lost none of its bonhomie in six years. "Scott Ballantine, you say? Jesus, we haven't handled him in years. There was this thing — anyway — what exactly are you looking for? We've got a coupla . . . say, who *is* this again?"

Ballantine hung up without answering. Maybe it would be easier in London — if he ever got there. He pulled a newspaper from the rack near the door and spread it out on the lunch counter. He was halfway through the bowl of chili when he saw the item. He put his fork down slowly and pinned the place with a forefinger. The by-line was Hollywood.

SEBASTIAN KYLE SIGNS FOR MAJOR PRODUCTION

Jules Levy announced the signing here today of veteran British director Sebastian Kyle. Kyle will direct the forthcoming Levy-Collins production of *Short Circuit*, Jody King's best-selling novel based on the Kyle tragedy of last year. Film rights are said to have sold for $240,000. San Channing scripts. Kyle was not available for comment at his Fairfax County home late last night.

Ballantine pushed his plate away. Then it *was* true. They had read the first rumors up in Springfield. Jordan had been right yet again, sure that Kyle wouldn't miss the chance of putting himself back in the big time. It was another reason why the Englishman wouldn't want a ghost from the past to materialize. He'd already had the publicity he needed. Ballantine called for his bill. What had been no more than a jailhouse dream was taking on solid proportions.

The counter clerk made change, cocking his head on one side at Ballantine's question.

"Communion of Saints? Sure. It's about half a mile out of town on Route 14. You can't miss it. There's some kind of a sign. Like nobody lives there now except Miz Palumbo. She's the caretaker."

Ballantine waved thanks and walked outside into the blinding sunshine. There was a vista of tree-shaded lawns and white-painted houses. This was still rural California. He turned east on a shimmering strip of hardtop, out of town through the citrus groves, his jacket over his shoulder. The sense of freedom was even stronger out here. It had something to do with the space and the trees. He reminded himself he could leave the road at any time and walk toward the hills till he lay down somewhere by water. That's what freedom meant and from now on he did as he pleased.

He stopped short at the cutoff. It dropped abruptly to a level twenty feet lower than the highway. A faded banner was stretched across the road, the lettering on it barely decipherable.

THE COMMUNION OF SAINTS
Prepare to meet thy God real soon!

He walked down the incline to what had once been a street. Paint peeled on the twenty-odd frame houses. The timber had been bleached the color of old bones. All the windows except one were boarded up. This was in a store with a tall false front. The glass there was still intact. A couple of fly-spotted photographs stood behind it. The blank faces of two elderly men stared out through the dirty window. A legend under each frame identified the subjects as

THE AVENGER   THE WITNESS

The hamlet lay in hot silence, a page out of Rip Van Winkle. Weeds grew up between the porch blanks, bright with butterflies. The occasional sound of a car passing above was almost lost. He picked his way through the soft dust. The street came to an abrupt end, overrun by a tangle of poison ivy. A small house on the left had been newly painted. Lavish use of water had kept the patch of grass green. A black Volkswagen glittered like a beetle in its carport. He saw the curtains move as he walked up the flagstone path. The door was thrown open before he had a chance to use the buzzer.

A thin woman with stick legs thrust into diamanté trousers was looking at him. She was wearing a white lace top. Her shoulder-length gray hair was tied back with a ratty piece of ribbon.

"Yes?" she snapped.

He smiled at her winningly. "I'm Scott Ballantine."

She stayed right where she was in the middle of the doorway. "That's nice."

He was hot and his throat was caked with dust. "I'm a friend of Brady's," he amplified. *An accomplice,* he should have said, *playing Friar Tuck to your nephew's Robin Hood.*

Her lipstick looked as if it had been applied in the dark. She sniffed.

"Where do you know him from? Hollywood?"

"That's right," he nodded.

She pointed along the porch. A couple of cane chairs were set there and, incredibly enough, a case of beer covered with dry ice.

"Help yourself," she said. "And fix one for me."

He knocked the caps off two bottles and looked around for glasses. There were none. Bracelets rattled up her skinny arm as she tilted the bottle. She drank like a woman who was accustomed to the maneuver. He cleared his throat hesitantly.

"I understand Brady told you I was coming." That had to be the understatement of the year.

She sat there inspecting him closely, grotesque in the green eye shadow.

"He told me. You don't look to me like a man who'd lend my nephew eighteen hundred dollars."

Jordan had warned that his aunt was kooky, but this woman was straight out of the witch scene in *Macbeth*. The boyish smile was getting him nowhere.

"You should have seen me last year, ma'am. I guess I presented a more prosperous appearance."

Mrs. Palumbo's herb cigarette stank like a bush fire. "Brady's in jail," she said flatly. "Gets out the day after tomorrow. He'll be coming here just the same as you did. Why couldn't he have given you the money then?"

She blew a stream of smoke at him and he coughed. His eyes were watering. Her own seemed impervious to the noisome cloud. He gestured at the case of beer, asking permission. He sent the second bottle to join the first and wiped his eyes and mouth.

"It's a long story, ma'am, and I don't think it would interest you. The main thing is that I need that money right now — today. But if you'd rather I come back when Brady's here . . ." Jordan had rehearsed him in the phony departure and suggested return.

She shook her head hurriedly. "I don't want you around here a second longer than's necessary, young man. I'll tell you something else, too. I don't want you hanging around my nephew anymore. If eighteen hundred dollars is going to get people like you off his back, it'll be the first money that he's spent wisely in a long while." She pulled a Bank of America envelope from her pants' pocket and gave it to Ballantine. "Count it," she ordered.

The bills were new and in sequence. The feel of them gave him fresh confidence. He stood.

"Thanks for the beer, ma'am. Tell Brady I'll call him."

She sprang up, glaring at him. "You'll do no such thing. Anything you have to say you can tell me. You a pot smoker too?"

He lifted a hand, his face solemn. "I'm a single man of unblemished character. I sing lead tenor in our local choir and I'm a member of the Volunteer Fire Brigade."

She smiled and was serious again as quickly. "You're a rogue and I wouldn't trust you an inch. Brady's a good boy and he's been through a lot. You give him the chance he deserves, hear? You'll have me to reckon with if you don't."

Her sincerity gave him a feeling of uneasiness. There was something indomitable about her in spite of her eccentricity. But if his heart bled for every little old lady with a case of beer on her front porch he'd be a cooked goose. She was Jordan's problem, anyway.

"Thanks . . ." he started again. The screen door banged, making the rest of the sentence useless. And that, he thought, was that.

It was past one by the time he walked back into town. The rush for the diners and lunch counters had siphoned off most of the activity. The streets were empty. He located the used car lots behind the bus depot. A banner over the nearest identified the owner as

FATSO YOUR FRIENDLY FARMER

A double line of cars was parked out front. The asking prices were scrawled on each windshield. He stepped onto the lot and looked the vehicles over. The part he had to play called for something cheap and inconspicuous. He walked around a '64 Chevrolet, trying to look as if he knew what he was doing. The chrome was yellowed in places. A rear fender showed evidence of repair. The tires were good. The tag on the black sedan was $750. The ignition keys dangled from the dashboard. He settled himself behind the wheel and hit the motor. The sudden roar brought a sharply dressed character to the door of the nearby office. He shaded his eyes like a baseball umpire flighting a line drive. He located the source of the noise and came hurrying toward it. He was wearing a silk shirt with his initials worked on his chest. He was fat, wore a toupee, and nothing like a friendly farmer. He pushed his head through the window, his voice admiring.

"Best value on the lot and you hit it in one. You sure have an eye!"

Ballantine switched off the motor. "There's enough carbon around these piston rings to filter Lake Malibu."

"Carbon!" The salesman laughed hollowly. "You have to be kidding, buddy! I want to tell you that this car belonged to a schoolteacher over in Santa Barbara. *There's* a doll! The only reason she turned it in was because she wanted something less lively."

Ballantine opened the glove compartment. He dug through the litter inside. The haul was intriguing: some gas station receipts, a stub for a seat at the fights, a card advertising a San Francisco burlesque show. He moved his head from side to side in mock wonder.

"A doll, huh?" Someone ought to put the P.T.A. on to her."

The salesman was unabashed. His laugh filled the inside of the car with the smell of cloves. "I can't mess with you. Seven-two-five and you drive her away. The rubber's new." Ballantine started climbing out through the door. The salesman caught him by the sleeve. His fingers moved up to the Canadian's elbow. "A full tank and a month's insurance. My own brother I couldn't do more for."

Ballantine removed the man's fingers. "I'll take it."

The salesman's voice changed. He bawled across the lot. A Negro in white overalls appeared from behind a billboard.

"Put twelve in the Chevy, Frank," the salesman shouted, "and wipe off those goddamn windows!"

He ushered Ballantine into the shack that served as office. There was just enough room for a table and two chairs. A list of hot cars hung under a girlie calendar. The man started drawing up a bill of sale. He pecked at the typewriter with blunt fingers. He looked up from the Canadian's driving license, his eyes reflective.

"Scott Ballantine! Sounds kinda familiar."

Ballantine took the bank envelope from his pocket. It was over six years since his arrest. Nobody's memory could be that long, not in California. He counted out eight crisp bills and spread them out on the table.

"Make it as fast as you can, will you? I've got a long drive ahead."

The salesman gathered the papers and money. "You

betcha. I'll just have to go next door. Ed Nolan handles the insurance. I'll be right back."

He was out of the room before Ballantine had time to answer. The salesman ducked through the wire that separated his car lot from his neighbor's. An insurance shield hung outside the office there. The Negro dragged out a hose and played it on the sedan. Ballantine watched him idly. Maybe if he shopped around he might have found a better bargain. There was no certainty. The used car market was a lottery. The main thing was that he'd found the sort of car that nobody would remember.

A police siren sounded in the neighboring lot. The noise took Ballantine to the window. The salesman was talking to a man in olive green trousers and a white Stetson. The sheriff nodded impatiently. They negotiated the wire and headed for the doorway where Ballantine was standing. The sheriff's shoulders blocked any further exit. The weathered skin on his neck was angry with razor nicks. He used a large hand to push the Canadian back into the office. He opened the other fist on Ballantine's papers and the eight hundred dollars.

"All this yours, son?"

The salesman was keeping well behind the sheriff, his eyes on the eight hundred dollars. Ballantine smiled nervously. This time he was making no mistakes.

"Sure thing, Sheriff."

The big man's inspection was slow and thorough. It took in the dust on Ballantine's shoes, lingered on the length of his hair.

"You carrying any other identification, son?" he asked.

107

Again with the 'son'! The sheriff's holster flap was un-buttoned and Ballantine moved to his pockets guardedly. Maybe it was against the law to walk in this part of the state. He offered his citizenship papers, added his birth certificate.

"Do you mind if I ask what this is all about, Sheriff?"

The officer's smile was patient, as if he'd heard the same question too many times. "I don't mind, no. A stranger comes into town and pays eight hundred dollars for a car in new bills — consecutive numbers. Well, we like to know a little more about him. You got any more of this money on you, son?"

Ballantine shrugged and gave him the Bank of America envelope. The sheriff came off the wall and picked up the phone. Ballantine sat down hard. His mouth was very dry. He could have taken a bus to Los Angeles and found a car on any one of five hundred lots. But no, General Jordan had to make it Palamos.

The sheriff's stubby finger dialed the number on the bank envelope. He was checking through Ballantine's identi-fication as he spoke.

"This is Sheriff Thornton — let me speak to Sam Locatelli. Sam? Listen I've got a bunch of your money here, eighteen new C bills. I'll read you the serial numbers." He did so, holding the receiver between his chin and shoulder. "Kosher, huh?" he said finally. He let the phone drop on the hook. He swung his chair around so that he faced Bal-lantine.

"You know Miz Palumbo good, son?"

The Canadian hedged. "Why don't you call her?"

Thornton was working on a tooth with a match. He suspended the operation to answer. "The bank already did. She claims that her nephew owes you this much money. Is that right?"

"That's right," said Ballantine.

Thornton spat the splinters of chewed wood from his mouth. "I've known Brady Jordan ever since he could walk. Eighteen hundred dollars is one helluva lot of dough for a guy sitting in the pokey to give up. You knew he was in jail?"

"I knew." As long as he kept his head, Ballantine reasoned, there was nothing this apple knocker could do — short of downright villainy.

The sheriff seemed to be making up his mind. He finally pushed money and papers back across the table. He hauled himself to his feet and looked down at the Canadian.

"Get yourself and that car out of town, son. I don't want to see you around here no more. OK?"

"OK," answered Ballantine. He threw in a look of injured innocence for good measure.

The salesman went as far as the wire with the sheriff. He came back, spreading his arms like an operatic tenor. "Don't look at me, old buddy. They got us guys over a barrel. There's a hundred and one things we're supposed to report. A couple of guys hit the First National Bank over in Sonora last year. They came through here and bought themselves a Cadillac. Blew it up in a roadblock at the Mexican border. It left Charley Thornton with a lot of headaches."

Ballantine was unimpressed. He left the eight hundred dollars lying and picked up the rest. "They ought to give you a tin badge," he said drily.

The salesman made change and put the bill of sale and

insurance policy in a plastic folder. His face was sheepish.

"Try living in a hick town like this. They're all on your back. If it isn't the law it's the sanitation department. Seems like nobody likes a used car lot."

"You can include me," said Ballantine, "and get it set to music." He walked through the door. The Chevrolet looked almost presentable. The Negro was wiping off the last of the water. Ballantine flipped him a dollar and took the wheel. Two brushes with the law in one day was too much for a guy in his position. Fortunately Mrs. Palumbo seemed to have kept her opinion of him to herself. Probably for Brady's sake. Apparently the sheriff was a friend of hers. There'd been that bit about knowing Jordan since he was in knee pants. Brady must have been out of his mind, anyway, sending him to a small town like this.

He collected his bag and drove north of U.S. Highway 101. He kept in the right lanes, operating the car with care to get the feel of the controls again after six years. The motor did everything he asked of it. At Salinas he forked west, on past Spreckles and headed for the coast. It was late afternoon when he reached Pacific Ramparts. The small town looked like a *Saturday Evening Post* cover. Banks of rosebushes separated the traffic lanes on the main street. There were no billboards, no television antennas.

He slowed to a crawl, looking for the real estate office Jordan had told him about. He found it on a block near Fisherman's Wharf, a two-story building with white stucco, arches, and a red roof. An MG roadster was parked out front. He eased the Chevrolet in behind it and rapped on the office door. An improbable ash blonde looked up over mauve-framed spectacles. She wore an assortment to pop jewelry over a kind of smock. The gothic lettered sign on her desk proclaimed her name: RONA REYNOLDS.

He gave her the benefit of a full frank smile. "Hi! You look like the sort of girl who could help me. I'm down here on a fishing vacation. I'm looking for a place on the beach. Las Rosas, if that's possible."

She touched the back of her hair self-consciously, sneaking another look at him.

"Would that be to rent? We don't handle too much rental business, Mr. . . . ?"

"Ballantine," he supplied. "Scott Ballantine."

She tried it once in silence. "Does it have to be in Las Rosas? There are places here in town."

He tried to make her part of his enthusiasm. "This probably won't mean too much to you but they tell me the fish run better out at Las Rosas than anywhere south of Pomponio, Mrs. Reynolds."

"Miss," she corrected. She shivered a little as if his words had conveyed some hidden compliment. She took off her spectacles.

"There is one place. It belongs to the dentist here in town. He only uses it in July and August. How long would you want it for?"

"A month. As from today."

She smiled shortsightedly. "Doctor Carberry's a bachelor. I've never been inside the place but I wouldn't expect much in the way of comfort."

He grinned. "I'm a bachelor, too. When you're on a fishing trip you don't worry too much about comfort, Miss Reynolds."

She picked up the phone and spoke for a few minutes. "You're in business. That was Doc Carberry himself. He'll let the beach house go for the month of June. One hundred dollars in advance and the electricity and phone are extra."

He took the money from his pocket, making his voice casual. "I only flew down from Canada today. I hope you're not going to ask for references. It'll take time."

She made a face and put her spectacles on again. "For Doc Carberry's place! I could tell you something about references anyway, Mr. Ballantine. We had a couple here last fall from Vermont. She was — well I'd better keep *that* to myself. Anyway, he was a minister's son. We checked his references out and it was true. What I mean is that it didn't stop him taking off with a whole truckload of somebody else's furniture. If it's OK with Doc Carberry, it's certainly all right with us. I'll have to ask you for another hundred dollars, though, Mr. Ballantine. Deposit against the utility bills. You going to be alone out there?"

He was conscious of her not-too-covert inspection. "I guess so," he answered. "A guy might be coming up for a day's fishing later. Someone I know down south."

"It seems such a waste." There was a hint of desperation in her coyness. "You wouldn't be interested in the theater by any chance? Our Rampart Players Club has a lot to offer and you certainly have the appearance."

"Just the fishing," he said politely.

She sighed. "It's always the same. Ah well. I'd better start closing up store. You'll find your house easily enough. There are only four of them. Yours is the last on the right. Don't take your car onto the beach, and burn your garbage. There's an ordinance against dumping. Have fun!"

He took the key she gave him. She was watching him from the window as he climbed into the car. She lifted a hand and he waved back. Maybe he should wear something on his back. People seemed to spend a great deal of time looking at it. He drove into a Farmer's Market and bought himself provisions — Scotch, beer, and a carton of groceries. The store was carrying a line of swimming trunks. He bought a pair, seeing himself lolling by the side of the Kyle pool. Las Rosas was well posted out of town. The narrow strip of hardtop finished in a pine wood that fringed the beach. He drove the Chevrolet into the trees and left it there. A few yards' walk took him to the beach. Tar balls, driftwood, and plastic containers marked the high water line. The beach was half a mile long, a crescent of golden sand locked in by tall wooded bluffs. The four houses differed largely in size and design. The one he had rented was the smallest. He took off his shoes and socks and started across the sand, carrying the box of groceries. His bare toes broke the hard crust. The line he was taking brought him close to all four houses. None of them showed signs of occupation. This came as no surprise. It was June; the kids were still at school. Jordan had said that the beach huts were only used during the day and on weekends. His description of the Kyle place was accurate, down to the surfboards hanging on the back porch.

He went up the steps on impulse. The windows were

113

shut but he could see through a chink in the living room curtains. The vases held fresh roses. He saw a studio couch and hi-fi set. There were pictures of Kyle as a younger man — leaning against an old-fashioned camera boom, posing on a horse with Charles Laughton. A plaque on the wall commemorated a screen directors' award. The date on it was 1948.

He walked along the porch and around to the bedroom. The curtains here were drawn tight. He tried to set the scene as it must have been a year ago. The deserted beach would have been bleach white under the moon when Jordan came through the pines. The woman had been lying here dead in this room, not long before his friend reached the house. The detectives testified that they had been right behind him. They claimed that they'd waited no more than five minutes — long enough to give the guilty parties time to stage the clinch needed for the cameras. Medical evidence had established no more than an approximate time of death. It could have happened any time during the fifteen minutes before Jordan's arrival. The state had attached great importance to the defendant's apparent indifference at the scene of the crime. A woman had been found dead — strangled — and he'd been the first to find her. And he'd done nothing about it, not even picked up the phone and called for help. According to his own account he'd just stood there, unable to move or think.

Ballantine believed it. Jordan was the kind of guy who'd stand there as the minutes stretched and then suddenly panic. He must have been literally generating guilt when the operatives burst in the door.

114

The porch out front was screened at both ends. A pair of canvas shoes was lying on the steps, their rope soles turned up to the sun to dry. He looked out to sea. Long rollers were invading the bay. They broke in creaming lines of surf that left the sand flattened and glistening. He swung around, hearing the call of a bird. He traced the sound to the pine woods. A small hawk was hanging high in the air, beating its wings, surveying the ground for prey. The hawk, the deserted beach, the complete and utter loneliness of everything stirred a deep sense of belonging. It was a feeling of satisfaction, as valid now as it had been twenty years ago. He found himself remembering the trees at home, the last of the winter's snow dripping from the branches under a pale Ontario sun. The air would be cold enough for his pony's breath to rise in clouds of steam. He still recalled the sharp sweaty smell of the tack room. The sprawling house was built of oak logs that his great-grandfather had hauled seventy miles. More sensory impressions clamored for recognition. The snug warmth throughout the long dark months — snow shifting on the roof — the few family portraits blackening in the smoke from the great open fireplace. He'd had his chance there, too. The last of the Ballantines and now the house was gone, its four hundred acres of fruit trees uprooted. A new township stood in their place. He smiled wryly, detecting the ham in himself. The truth was that the pages of the past were glued together. You could never turn back except in the mind.

He walked on fifty yards to the house he had rented. It was no more than a shack built of raw timber. The doors and window frames were warped by salt and sun. He negotiated a porch that was perilous with rusted rings of bait hooks. He used the key, narrowing his nose at the dank smell of disuse. The lights worked; the phone responded with a dialing tone. There were only three rooms: a living room, a place to sleep, and a tiny kitchen with an old-fashioned wood stove. He threw the back door wide, dislodging a colony of roaches. There was an incinerator at the bottom of the porch steps. The furniture looked as if Doctor Carberry were an amateur carpenter. The two beds were laid on trestles. He found a pile of blankets and sheets in a closet. He carried an armful out into the sunshine to dry. It was a quarter to seven. He stripped down to his shorts and sat on the front steps with pencil and paper. He made a list of what he had spent of Jordan's money. He noted no more than the price of the car and the rent. He'd eat and drink on his own time as long as the meager supply of cash lasted.

He emptied a can of chopped clams, boiled milk, and made himself a chowder. He connected the icebox, drinking his Scotch as his father had done — water, no ice. He took his meal out on the steps again and lifted the glass to his mouth. The almost forgotten flavor rolled over his tongue, warming his belly. The Kyle house fascinated him. He looked at it, munching, trying to solve Jordan's riddle. The state had tried and failed — had given up interest at any rate. There was nothing really to do but go along with Jordan's version. He dropped the dishes in the sink and went to bed without even turning on the light.

Habit waked him at seven. He opened a cautious eye.

The room was even shabbier in the early morning sunshine. He rolled out of bed and went to the window. The tide had washed the beach clean. Amber sand shaded into gold, untouched by a single footstep. He shuddered at the thought of going into the water. He had a country man's dread of the ocean. He was boiling an egg when he heard a car being driven into the pine woods. He reached the kitchen window in time to see a tan-colored station wagon nosing its way through the trees. A girl appeared at the tailgate. She took something out then started down across the beach, followed by a wire-haired terrier. She began running as he watched. One hand was clutching a basket, the other her hair. She was wearing the briefest of shorts, her sunburned legs flashing. Her paisley shirtwaist was knotted across her bare midriff. The clump-cut hair and small breasts gave her a boyish appearance. But she ran like a girl, knock-kneed with her bottom swinging.

He recognized her immediately from the courtroom pictures. It was Kyle's daughter. She unlocked the beach house and went inside. The dog scampered off along the sand, running in ever-narrowing circles. Ballantine shaved in the tiny bathroom, keeping an eye on his neighbor. She was out of the house again before he had finished breakfast. Her brown body was surprisingly shapely in a polka-dot bikini. Her head was bare. She carried one of the surfboards to the edge of the water, jumped onto it, kneeling, and paddled it out with her hands. She was making for the north end of the bay where the rollers were coming in faster. The terrier followed her progress from the shore, barking.

Ballantine slipped out of the back door. It was barely after nine but the sand burned his bare feet. He was wearing the swimming trunks he'd bought in the supermarket. He headed for the shade of the pines. The rear of the Ford station wagon was littered with dog food and saddlery. The doors were unlocked. He lifted the flap of the glove compartment. An operator's license was in a plastic flap inside. He read the name and address:

> Antonia Kyle
> Oak Valley
> Route #28
> Fairfax County
> Calif.

He walked along the fringe of pines toward the northern bluff. The ground started to rise, gently at first then steeply. The sandy soil gave way to rock, pines to cypresses. He slapped a whining insect from his back, wondering why he wasn't wearing shoes and a shirt. His feet were already killing him. He climbed the arroyo till he reached the top. He was on a driveway that ran along the spine of the bluff to its crest. Anyone standing on it was out of sight from the beach except where a chain stretched across the road. The arroyo there was wider than the rest, oleanders clinging to the soil. The chain blocked the way to the house beyond. There was no mailbox, no shingle, no name.

He vaulted the chain, walked fifty yards, and then stopped. The low house perched on the edge of the bluff. Cypresses screened it on all sides except seaward. He went forward cautiously. The house was obviously unoccupied, the windows steel shuttered. A handrail sunk in cement protected the mirador. He craned over the edge of the cliff. Directly below was a flat shelf of rock. It was maybe fifty feet beneath the mirador. Tina Kyle was lying there on her back, completely naked. Her firm tiny breasts were paler cups against the deep tan of her body. Brown merged into cream below her navel, terminating in a shadowed V. She moved as he looked, without haste, completely sure of her privacy. He pulled back hurriedly as she rolled over on her stomach. The sight of her lying there revived every erotic memory he had had in six years. That part of his mind he'd kept secret, deaf to the bawdy bunkhouse reminiscences. He'd protected it, flashed-tempered to the point of violence.

He peeked again, in spite of himself. The girl was still on her stomach, her head pillowed on her surfboard. He was suddenly thirsty and walked back to the patio. A faucet was leaking sweet water. He drank deeply and wiped his mouth on his forearm. It must have been up here that Jordan had heard the car that night. And when he'd heard it, Joanne had been dead. It would have been no trick for a man to have scrambled down any one of the half-dozen arroyos gouging the side of the bluff. He tried the route himself, slithering on loose pebbles, braking by grabbing the oleander bushes. It was easy enough, he decided at the bottom. He found himself wondering why a woman wouldn't have been able to do it as well as a man.

He put on his clothes and drove into town, noting where the cutoff to the house on the bluff joined the highway. He parked the Chevrolet in front of the Community Center. This was a red brick building with barbered grass out front. He crossed the grass to read what was written on the notice board.

A Theatrical Presentation
in Aid of
the
Joanne Kyle Memorial Fund

SHE STOOPS TO CONQUER
Given by
The Rampart Players

He walked away hurriedly, fearful of meeting the woman from the agency. He found an army surplus store at the end of the flower-bordered street. He made a few purchases and carried them back to the car. It was late afternoon when he reached the pines. Tina Kyle's station wagon was still there. He unloaded the things he had bought: a cane fishing rod, a pair of light-weight Japanese binoculars, a large scale map of the county. He crossed the beach, closing his mouth against the heat that came off the sand. The terrier scented him a hundred yards away. It scampered toward him, stopped, stiff-legged and challenging. He did his best to ignore it, ready to swipe if it came at him from the rear. There was no sign of its mistress.

He let himself into his own place and slipped into the swimming trunks once more. Life at the camp had left his body brown. He sucked in his belly and hardened his pectorals, looking at himself in the square of mirror. The vital organs of a man ten years younger, Tamaru had said. Whatever it meant, it sounded good. He sat on the front porch for a while, the binoculars in his lap. Suddenly he leveled them. Something was moving at the base of the northern bluff. The surfboard flashed in the sunshine. Tina Kyle threw it well clear of the rocks. Her jackknife dive broke surface close to the board. She was up on it easily, first on one knee then erect, balancing gracefully. She came toward the shore traveling at twenty miles an hour and finished in a splash in the shallows. Ballantine dropped the glasses back in their case, impressed by the performance yet resentful of it. Tina Kyle's expertise reminded him of female karate experts, of highly coached brats with tennis serves like Pancho Gonzalez. Women should have the wit not to excel in this kind of area.

The girl came running across the sand, shaking the water out of her hair. He gave her five minutes and then walked over. She had changed into shorts and a halter and was lying on a towel spread on the front porch.

He called from the bottom of the steps. "Hi!"

The dog was by her side and snarled viciously. She kept her eyes closed. He tried again, giving her the old slow smile that had slain the technicians on Stage Eleven.

"Hi, there!"

She raised her head deliberately, keeping her hands clasped behind her neck. The maneuver flattened her stomach, he noticed, poking out the hard mounds of breasts above it. Her face was hardly beautiful. The shape was wrong for a start. The line from her ear to her chin was too long. She had a thin freckled nose and a sullen mouth. Her gray eyes were flecked like a tomcat's. It was the sort of face, he thought, that would force its way into your remembrance whether you wanted it or not.

121

"I'm out of matches," he called.

She was holding the dog firmly by the collar. "Inside on the windowsill. Take the box. I have more."

He stepped gingerly past the still-growling terrier. The girl was pointedly indifferent. The front door was open. Her wet bikini was lying over the back of a chair. He took a handful of stove matches.

"You ride a good board," he said, coming out again. "I was watching you."

She had a trick of intentness as she spoke, switching her gaze away at the end with a kind of contemptuous indifference.

"I noticed," she said shortly.

He put her age somewhere in the early twenties. There were lines at the corners of her mouth and eyes but her skin was fine textured.

Looking down at the angry animal, he moved his snapping fingers away hurriedly. "I'm Scott Ballantine. I'm living in the Carberry place for a month."

Her vowel sounds held a trace of British locution. "I don't want to appear rude but did you say you wanted matches or conversation?"

He leaned against the doorjamb, looking down at her. "Since you put it that way, both."

She lifted herself on her elbows. The sullenness spread to her eyes. "Then I think you've misunderstood me, Mr. Ballantine. I'll give you the benefit of the doubt, anyway. Please leave me alone."

He held his hand up hastily. "I'm on my way. Don't shoot."

He heard the porch door slammed shut long before he reached his own place. He poured himself a beer and carried it out to the steps. He heard the girl calling her dog. Shortly afterward the station wagon started up. He dropped his empty glass and took stock. Maybe he'd lost his touch — his hair was too long or something. He'd been polite enough, unless she was one of these oddballs who really *wanted* to be alone. That was something they'd never considered. The way things looked, getting invited by her was like getting invited by a sidewinder. So what now — apologize? But for what? All he could offer was the same ploy, a little bit better produced but essentially the same. He had a premonition that none of this was going to be as easy as Jordan had figured. The doubt left an odd taste in his mouth — no check, no money. He thought about this for a while. Another twenty-four hours and Jordan himself would be free. There was one guy who'd be expecting a lot more than was for offer at the moment.

He poured himself another beer, recognizing the familiar stubbornness that was creeping into his mind. He'd come too far to go back now, lived too long with a dream of *la dolce vita*. If he couldn't make the inside of the Kyle house in one way, he'd have to do it in another. He spread out the map on the living room table. Oak Valley lay beyond the Carmel River, fifteen miles away. He sipped his beer slowly, shaping a plan of campaign. For the second night in succession he went to bed without light. Sleep came less easily this time. The vision of a girl lying naked on a rock kept it at bay.

123

It was the next day and late morning with a relentless sun in a starched blue sky. The Chevrolet was parked in an orange grove off Route 28. He was sitting on the roof, dressed in slacks and a shirt. The binoculars were slung on a strap around his neck. The house he was watching was a thousand yards away. It presented its back to the road at this point, a low rambling structure with a rash of outbuildings. The only cover on the near side was a knee-high carpet of ferns. His two-hour vigil had given him a good idea of the layout. Post-and-rail fencing enclosed a hundred-acre paddock. There were stables attached to the garage. He could see a dense stand of oaks in front of the house, a pool with a diving board and canvas-topped swing. A driveway wound through the oak thicket, connecting with Route 28 at a point half a mile away. The vintage Rolls had left shortly after his arrival. He'd held the glasses on it, getting a momentary glimpse of a white-haired man with an imposing head. At first sight Kyle bore little resemblance to his daughter. His driving appeared to be as conventional as his car. He stopped dead at the empty highway, spending a good two minutes looking right and left before moving on. There was no show of activity in the house for the next hour or so. Then Tina Kyle had ridden out of the stables, jumped a flight of hurdles in the paddock, and cantered her horse out of sight. That had been at half-past nine. It was past eleven now.

The sound of hooves rattled on the highway. He clambered down from the roof and made for the road. He came out of the orange trees, emerging in the ditch almost under the horse's hindquarters. The bay stallion reared, pitching its rider forward. The suddenness of the move caught the girl off balance. Her jockey cap tilted over her nose. She scrambled back in the saddle, pulling her mount up on a tight rein. Ballantine stepped sideways smartly. The girl looked as if she were actually going to ride him down. She pushed up her jockey cap, her expression furious.

"Goddamn you, are you *completely* insane? Coming out of the ditch like that!"

He looked up at her warily. "I didn't see you — I'm sorry. You're riding too short by the way."

She checked the length of her stirrup leathers instinctively. She was wearing a checked cotton shirt with a silk scarf tied at the neck. Her white drill pants were streaked with dirt as if she had already fallen. Ballantine stepped out of the ditch. The stallion showed the whites of its eyes. The girl wrenched its head around, her mouth thin with anger.

"What are you doing here anyway?"

He gestured at the orange trees behind him. "Bird watching. There's no law against it, is there?"

She looked at his binoculars, rose in her stirrups, and rode a few yards. The glint in her eyes told him that she had seen the parked car. Her tone was dangerously quiet.

"Why are you following me?" she demanded. "Yesterday on the beach and now here."

He grinned peaceably. "It's a good question and I wish I could answer it. The truth is I was bird watching — like I told you."

Her neck and face flamed. "Then let me tell you something, Mr. Ballantine — if that really *is* your name! The moment I get back to the house, I'm going to call the Sheriff Department. You'll find that we have a way of dealing with people like you in this community."

His face sobered. "Now you've lost me. What sort of people am I supposed to be, Miss Kyle?"

A truck rounded the curve, barreling by, uncomfortably near. She pulled her horse to one side.

"How do you know my name?"

He caught the reins close to the bit, quietening the dancing stallion.

"I do other things besides bird watching. I fish, for instance, and I read. Newspapers, for instance."

She freed the reins from his grasp, smiling for the first time. "I suppose we'll be seeing more of one another since you're a neighbor?"

"I hope so," he said truthfully.

"In that case, we'd better call a truce." She leaned down, offering her left hand. As he reached up to take it, she staggered him with a backhanded blow across the mouth. His tongue tasted blood. She was still smiling. "The good neighbor policy, Mr. Ballantine."

She wheeled the stallion around and jumped the ditch. The powerful animal's hooves pounded through the dusty ferns. He licked his lips cautiously. The cut was on the inside of his mouth. His eyes were watering and his nose stung. He watched till horse and rider were out of sight. It was the first time he could remember taking a blow without retaliating. But then it was the first time that a woman had struck him. He'd make sure that it was the last. There were people who claimed that the experience could be exciting. His own feeling was one of plain hostility.

It was almost three o'clock by the time he reached home. He dialed the Palamos number. The answering voice was unmistakable.

"Daisy Palumbo."

"This is Scott Ballantine," he volunteered. "Could I talk to Brady, please?"

He heard her close a door, the jingle of her bracelets as she picked up the phone again.

"He's not here."

He looked away through the window, suddenly at a loss. Gulls were scavenging the empty beach. There was no one in the other houses.

"You mean he hasn't arrived?" he asked after a while.

There was a long pause. "You still on the line?" she asked sharply. "I mean he's not here."

He moved his head mechanically. "Do you want to tell me when you expect him, Mrs. Palumbo?"

Her voice was very distinct now. "Now you listen to me, young man. I know all about you and so does Sheriff Thornton. You're no good! I'm telling you keep away from Brady, hear?"

He put the phone down without answering her. She was running this sheriff thing into the ground. She had to be bluffing. Jordan would know how to handle her. There was a pile of old M.D. magazines. He browsed through them with interest for an hour then spread the map out. He retraced his movements that morning. One thing at least had

127

been resolved — he'd never be invited into the Kyle house now. That was all right, too. He went back in time to a summer evening in state prison, three years ago. Cell-blocks enclosed the dusty yard. Groups of men were squatting or wheeling in endless aimless procession. Base-balls smacked into catchers' gloves. The yard was noisy with the yells of the players. And sitting across the table had been Gerry Hunt.

The tall Texan had stepped off a plane from Houston in 1965, alone and completely unknown. For the next forty-two months he had run the Los Angeles Police Department off its feet. The bag he brought with him contained a spare seersucker suit, a complete set of Raymond Chandler novels, and various homemade picklocks and skeleton keys. In Houston he had been a smalltime burglar and second-story man. The coast had changed him into a will-o'-the-wisp flitting through the canyon houses, the privately policed estates in the hills. Sometimes he was a delivery man with flowers, a shill for a charitable institution, an inspector from the Department of Sanitation. He was a lanky well-dressed stranger driving a rented car and looking for a long-lost relative. His entrances and exits were made without fuss. Nothing was ever lost on these occasions. The action came later, sometimes as much as a month later. Five minutes inside a house was enough for him to assess any security precautions that had been taken. He learned about burglar alarms, electronic traps, direct lines to the local police precinct. He chose his victims from the social register. Invariably he waited in a garden, often up a tree, watching the house he was going to hit.

When the moment was right he moved. It became so that he could negotiate the dark with the sixth sense of a blind man. He extracted safe keys from beneath a sleeper's pillow with the delicacy of a mosquito. He never carried a weapon and stole three quarters of a million dollars worth of jewelry in a little short of four years. He was finally caught changing a wheel for the friend of a woman he had just robbed. The Texan's memories reflected certain principles for budding burglars.

Patience headed the list. Four hours up a tree, he declaimed in a laconic drawl, could sure skin the ass off you but that last light, man, could be the one that would do the dame. See that last light out and then wait some more. Keep away from houses with small babies living in them. Babies could mean unexpected risings during the night. The more sophisticated the owner, the less likely you were to find her jewelry hidden in exotic places. Break up the loot yourself, he said. Sell the stones a thousand miles away. Best of all, buy yourself a jewelry store as a cover.

Ballantine folded the map. *Patience.* The thought about his coming assault on the Kyle house gave him a definite feeling of excitement.

Sebastian G. Kyle   June 1970

HE TURNED OFF on the rise and up through the trees. The drive back from Hollywood had tired him. He was getting too old for the massed charge along the freeways, the constant preoccupation with Highway Patrolmen, the driving habits of the young. *Really* old, he reflected. Intolerance was a sign of age, Tina assured him, and above all he *was* intolerant.

The oak thicket came to an abrupt ending, as if a giant razor had shorn it off square with the currycombed grass. Gum trees grew on the lawn, planted to discourage the mosquitoes. The house was mercifully free of them, thank God. The two-story building rambled in a way that had always pleased his eye — an agglomeration of afterthoughts. Extra rooms had been added here and there as the previous owners' whims had taken them. Kyle secretly despised the subculture he worked in. He hated much about California and its inhabitants but this house was his home. *Ein fester Burg*, he thought. Its thick whitewashed walls were a refuge from everything except perhaps conscience.

He drove the Rolls into the three-car garage. He eyed his daughter's station wagon with disfavor. It looked like the inside of a hen coop. Filthy. He switched off the motor and reached behind for his dispatch case. He had brought the running script home with him to read. The studio conference had resolved into yet another unpleasant wrangle between the production unit and the writer. He'd sat through it all, deep in his chair. His manner for the occasion had been de-

131

veloped over the years — head bent, one hand covering his eyes. The pose protected him from anything but the direct question. At the same time it suggested an intelligent appreciation of whatever conversation was going on. Channing had lifted his script straight out of the trial record, of course. There was no attempt to disguise the principals. But they still used the jargon associated with imaginative writing. Channing was a weary sophisticate of thirty-two with one good credit locked away in his bank vault.

"Motivation," he'd said suddenly, playing with the end of his Charvet tie. He let the word drift the length of the conference table, a balloon to be caught. Nobody grabbed at it so Channing continued. "What makes a young and good-looking woman break her marriage vows? Don't give me this crap about 'themal elaboration.' *I'm* the writer! The whole goddamn story hangs on just that — her motivation. Unless this is crystal clear there *is* no story!"

An assistant producer with a ferocious crew cut explained the facts of life in a bored tone. "What's to make clear — the guy's ancient. She's getting it somewhere else."

There was an abrupt silence. Somebody coughed. Kyle took his hands away from his eyes.

"Don't mind me, gentlemen. My contract is a generous one. Mr. Kruse is perfectly right and expresses himself with his usual charm. The lady was indeed getting it elsewhere." Five minutes later he was on his way home.

He walked out of the garage, carrying his dispatch case. A mellowed brick wall separated the rose garden from the lawn. The evening breeze was heavy with the scent of the flowers. He opened the door and peeped in. The small en-

132

closure was the size of a tennis court. Every rosebush had been imported from England with the stone Peter Pan and the sundial. He sat there when his mind was tired. Bees hummed drowsily among the peach trees growing against the wall. There was an illusion of Devonshire, of the vicarage garden that was anchored in his memory.

He closed the door and went into the house through the drawing room. The shades had been drawn to protect his collection of Skeapings. The Bechstein grand had belonged to his first wife. No one had touched it since her death. The freshly cut flowers in the silver vase would be Mrs. Bruce. Tina had never cut a flower or thrown a dead blossom out in her life. He wondered what either of them would have done without the diminutive Scotswoman. She had been with them for eighteen years, producing balanced meals, sending his clothes to the cleaner's, answering Tina's letters from school. She drank a single glass of Chivas Regal every night and managed their affairs without fuss or extravagance. He poked his head into the kitchen. The housekeeper was sitting at the table reading a week-old copy of the *Scotsman*. The years on the coast had warmed her smooth skin to the color of a ripe peach. She had a mist of gray hair and still dressed in the soft browns of her native Hebrides. She looked up, holding her place with a forefinger.

"You're home early, sir. I'd intended dinner for nine. Miss Tina said you'd be later." She had no time for the easy familiarity of the country she was living in and called him "sir" habitually. Her own quarters were next to the kitchen. A bedroom and sitting room and bath opened onto a small terrace patrolled by her one-eared cat.

133

He smiled. "I got away sooner than I expected, Mrs. Bruce. Where *is* Tina?"

"She was in your study, sir."

The wide corridor split the house lengthways. His study was at the other end of the house. A central staircase curved up to the second story. He had bought the place for fifty-two thousand dollars back in 1943. The following day he had caught a plane for Lisbon. The sad-eyed ballerina he brought back to share his home stayed in it just long enough to produce a daughter. Fanny Kyle's return to England had been a jail break in every sense of the word. She hated motherhood, the loss of her figure, and her stay in the United States in that order. Toward the end she was hating the man who was responsible for all three. A V-1 rocket dropped out of a clear Kent sky one evening and put an end to her problems. Her portrait hung on the stairs, a slim woman in a tutu with eyes that haunted those who passed. Everything she had cared for and left had been preserved — her piano, a signed photograph of Nijinsky, a pair of coral earrings that had been Pavlova's. Tina's memory of her mother was colored by what Kyle had told her. She never knew that she had been deserted. On the contrary, she had grown up with a romantic belief in Fanny Kyle's flashing career and dramatic death.

He came into the study quietly. He kept his books and papers here, otherwise the word was a misnomer. French windows overlooked the pool outside. Another Skeaping hung above the open fireplace — a blue-and-white study of horses in the Camargue. He'd let Tina put in a new carpet shortly after the trial; it was a ridiculous shade of blue and already scarred by cigarette burns.

His daughter was lying on the sofa clad in a halter and shorts. Her legs were drawn up under her. He bent down and put his face against hers. She had been sleeping when he left in the morning. She circled his wrist with tanned fingers.

"How did it go, darling?"

He emptied the dispatch case on his desk. "Like any other studio conference. It was a discussion in depth by opinionated men ignorant of their subject. They've finished casting — or as good as — we ought to start shooting in a month's time."

He opened the walnut highboy. Concealed lights came on inside. He hesitated in his choice of bottle then settled for Campari. He sliced lemon, added vermouth, ice, and soda water. He carried his drink to the sofa. She made room for him, lifting her own glass from the floor and saluting him with it. He drained his drink gratefully and patted his lips with his handkerchief.

"All right," he demanded. "What is it?"

She swung her bare feet into his lap. "What is *what?*"

"The face. I know when something's wrong."

She wriggled her toes in his fingers. "I lost my temper this morning and clobbered a would-be admirer. I mean *virtually* clobbered."

He smiled, vaguely appeased. Her admirers never lasted for long. He was under no illusion that she was a virgin. He was equally sure that her heart had never been involved. Her heart was his, it was as simple as that. The extent of their love for one another was known to them only. His gaze was fond.

"Who was it this time, anyone I know?"

The smile faded, leaving her eyes hard. "A gentleman calling himself Ballantine. He's taken Doctor Carberry's beach house for a month. He made himself known yesterday afternoon. Nothing very subtle — the usual kind of thing — did I have a match? Then this morning he was up on the road behind the paddock. With a pair of field glasses."

He lifted her legs out of his lap, suddenly chilled. He crossed to the cabinet and fixed himself another drink. He swirled the ice in the glass thoughtfully.

"Field glasses. What was he doing with them?"

She followed him to the highboy, walking barefooted, "Watching me, I imagine. He said he was bird watching. He didn't seem to care too much whether I believed him or not."

"I think I'll call Carberry," he decided.

She took his fingers away from the phone. "I already have. He's a Canadian on a fishing holiday. At least that's what he told the agency." Her head was in the drinks cabinet. "You sound worried, Daddy!"

He fired the word back at her, covering his disturbance with a show of anger. "Of course I'm worried! And I wish you wouldn't walk around the house like that, Antonia, half naked."

She cocked her head. "*Antonia!* Don't tell me it's as bad as that!"

She had the same stylized grace as her mother when she walked. She sat down beside him.

"What is it, sweetheart?"

"Jordan was released from jail this morning. You know that as well as I do."

Her eyes clouded. "I'd honestly forgotten. Does it matter? I mean, do you think there's some connection between him and this Ballantine?"

His mind and his conscience had long ago accepted the myth of her mother's departure. Other than that he'd lied to her once — that long night over a year ago. And then he'd been lying for them both. His voice was quiet.

"I've got a feeling that they might be going to reopen the case."

She sat very still, twisting the amethyst ring on her finger. She aimed the words at a point between her bare feet.

"Why did you let them talk you into making this film, Father?"

That at least was a question that he could answer. "Because I hadn't worked for over two years for a start. And they'd have made it without me anyway. I've been all through this with Marcus, at length. If I'd sued Levy it would have been tantamount to a retrial in a civil court with every piece of dirt they could dredge up thrown at us."

She lifted her thatch of sun-streaked hair. "Then I don't understand. Why should they want to open the case again now?"

He moved his shoulders resignedly. "The file in a murder case is never closed."

She found him with a swift sideways glance. "Whom would they suspect?"

He avoided the direct reply. "You were there. You heard Donatelli's suggestions in open court. Nobody stopped him from making them. I had every right to ask for police protection and they fob me off with some nonsense about hay barns being burned. I have a feeling that this fellow living

137

in Carberry's place could be some sort of detective."

The heat of the day lay across the room in swaths of golden sunlight. Yet she shivered.

"That woman's poisoning our lives even now. And you wondered why I hated her."

The bitterness in her tone recalled the agony of the day he had brought his second wife back to Oak Valley. Joanne had matched her stepdaughter's outraged iciness with the confidence of a woman who is certain that she must win the battle. But it promised to be a long one. Tina seemed to sense the coming tragedy, drawing closer to him in the mockery of the following months. Not once was she drawn to comment on her stepmother's constant absences. She waited till the night he returned from London. Joanne hadn't been in the house to greet him. A thin-lipped Mrs. Bruce explained that his wife was at the beauty parlor. It was a quarter to ten at night and the housekeeper's disbelief was obvious. Once they were alone, Tina produced a clipping from a Hollywood scandal sheet. It was written in the style of the medium and headed

FOR WHOM THE BELL TOLLS?

Spies along the Strip prattle about the end of yet another June and December match. The ever-loving wife of one of our senior directors is being seen more and more in the company of swains younger than her mate. Discretion marks the lady's choice of venues for her adventures. Rumor names a Nordic sportsman as the lucky cavalier. The odds givers are asking when the penny will drop upstate.

The memory was painful. He held his daughter tight for a second. "I'm sorry, darling. I hope it's not too late to say it?"

138

She padded to the corridor and shut the door. Her voice trembled a little in the gentle sounds of the evening. "I love you more than anything else in this world, Father. Enough to be trusted with the truth. Who *did* kill Joanne?"

The unvoiced question he had seen in her eyes a hundred times had come at last. He moved his heavy shoulders.

"Levy's got the highest-priced writer in the business working on the problem. He still hasn't resolved it. This film will fall flat on its face unless he does. As far as I can understand, the choice lies between a teen-age sex maniac and myself."

Her look for him was compassionate. "You didn't answer my question. I'm *glad* that she's dead, do you understand! It's just that I can't bear to see you suffer like this."

He pulled her down into his lap. She was a small girl again and afraid. He held her very tight.

"You think I know who did it, don't you?"

She twisted her head and nodded. Tears brimmed and rolled. She brushed them away angrily.

"You're protecting someone. I've felt it ever since that night. I want to know *who*. I've *got* to know to be able to protect you. Can't you see that?"

The tenderness in her eyes stirred him. To continue lying to her was the worst betrayal of all.

"Trust me, darling," he begged. "You must. When the time comes I'll tell you everything. Meanwhile I'm as frightened as you are. Jordan's a vengeful man. I've got a feeling he might be making trouble with the police."

She pulled herself away and lit a cigarette. "To do what? And why should he bother with me?"

139

It was difficult to reveal danger without giving a valid reason for it.

"I told you. You've got to trust me, Tina."

She blew smoke nervously. "I always have but it works both ways, Father."

The ice in his glass had watered. He finished the drink slowly.

"It's true. I don't have the right to lie to you. I *do* know who killed Joanne. But if it ever comes out it'll be the finish of me."

It was her turn to comfort him. "Nobody's going to harm you, darling. Whatever was done was done for me. That bitch had no place in our life. I'd have killed her myself, gladly."

He found himself weeping. Like an old man. There no longer should be any need for tears for either of them. He remembered what he'd said to her many years ago — reassurance to a thirteen-year-old beset by circumstances. *There's nothing we can't face together — nothing!* He had meant it then and believed it now. He smiled across the room, lifting an arm solemnly.

"I'll never ask you to do anything that you don't feel is right, Tina. This is a promise. Will you remember that?"

She was herself again now, a creature of steel and whalebone. "That and a million other things, sweetheart. If Ballantine worries you, put the bird dogs on him. Call Kowalsky."

"I'd rather not talk about it anymore," he replied. He looked from his watch to the script open on the desk. The hell with it. They'd sit together in the rose garden after din-

ner, the backgammon board between them. The fierceness
of her loyalty had given him new courage to tell her the
truth. But courage wasn't enough.

She opened the door, calling to the housekeeper that they
were coming to eat. Her question to him was casual.

"What am I supposed to do about this man? He's living
on the beach. Do you want me to keep away?"

The effort of rising was a result of too many meals eaten in
studio cafeterias.

"For the moment, nothing."

"What does that mean — do I go to the beach or not?"

He took her arm. "I want you to carry on as if nothing
had happened. I don't suppose he'll try again but if he does
you're well equipped to deal with him."

She tightened her muscle on his fingers. "Suppose that
he isn't a policeman?"

He filled his lungs with the smell of the waiting food.
"Then perhaps we'll have a surprise for him," he said lightly.
The boast had less logic in it than hope.

Brady Jordan   June 1970

THE TRAIN RATTLED over the points by the silo yards. Jordan stuck his head out of the window as the conductor came into the day coach calling the familiar name. It was years since he had ridden into town like this. The depot was precisely as he recalled it. The long bank of scarlet-and-green geraniums spelled out the name

PALAMOS

The more cunning of the town's stray dogs were lying over on the shady side of the tracks. They'd move with the first freight train to scavenge in back of the bunkhouse. The usual group of train watchers was in position outside the Western Union office.

The coach swung into the last curve. He could see his aunt waiting out in the station concourse. She was wearing what looked like a Vietnam peasant outfit — drab trousers under a gaudy smock, a cone-shaped coolie hat. She was talking to a man in a sheriff's uniform. Jordan pulled in his head and picked his bags up. It wasn't easy to imagine Aunt Daisy in love, let alone soft in womanly surrender. Yet it had once been true, twenty years ago or more. Charley Thornton had held office since he was thirty-five, a sharp-witted man with something of Jimmy Stewart about him. He was respected beyond politics, was the town's hottest shot with a billiard cue, and ran his bailiwick calmly and efficiently. He'd caught Aunt Daisy on the rebound, a couple

143

of years after her husband's death. Their affair had flared briefly. Neither of them seemed to have had the will or nerve to carry it beyond the few months that it lasted. From that time on they treated one another with an affectionate familiarity that had long since passed into local acceptance. If Daisy had one real friend it was Thornton and vice versa.

Jordan swung himself down from the coach and walked through the waiting room. His aunt and Thornton saw him at the same time. Jordan caught the tiny woman and lifted her off her feet. He swung her around before putting her down. Thornton's hand was outstretched.

"Good to see you, Brady."

The top half of Mrs. Palumbo's face was hidden under her hat. All Jordan could see was a determined chin and a mouth that had been put on lopsidedly. She fingered his travel-stained shirt, clucking disapprovingly.

"What's the matter with your manners these days — don't you put a tie on even to meet your aunt?"

He smiled at her fondly. "Not when she's wearing trousers. Hi, Charley!"

Thornton's uniform was ancient but spotless. A mesh of broken veins marred the end of his leathery nose. His cheeks were scraped to a cornstarch polish. His hazel eyes weighed Jordan in the balance for a few seconds.

"Your aunt's a good woman, Brady. Treat her right — OK?" He'd put himself on show deliberately for the benefit of the kibitzers peering out of the drugstore window. The sheriff looked for no justification beyond that of his conscience.

"Will do, Charley," said Jordan.

144

The sheriff's car was parked twenty yards away. He glanced across at it, clearing his throat.

"What about your parole officer — when are you going to check in?"

Jordan wrapped an arm around his aunt and held her close. "Monday. He left a message at Springfield. He's up in Sacramento."

His aunt moved impatiently. "Then let's get out of here. Ray Leadbitter's just about falling through his store window and you've got work to do, Charley Thornton. Go lock someone up!"

Thornton opened the door for her. "It could be you, Daisy. You're a traffic hazard in those trousers."

Mrs. Palumbo's sniff hid her pleasure. She settled behind the wheel, sitting on a cushion. She drove with her chin pointing in the direction she was taking. Jordan's gaze was on the street. Coming back like this was an anticlimax — the end of the Jordan legend. A sort of folklore had grown up about him in the small town. He was the envy of every kid under twenty-five — the sophisticate whose name sometimes showed on the credits when the lights went out in Kahn's Palace of Varieties. He was their link with the outside world, a constant point of argument for the rebels fretting for the big city.

He grabbed the top of the open window as the Volkswagen balked at the town's one set of traffic signals.

"What's all this with Charley?" he asked idly. "You're a good guy — I'm a good guy. What's he selling?"

She leaned on the horn ring. "Don't bother me while I'm driving!" A truck driver filtered through against the red.

"Bum!" yelled Aunt Daisy. She winced as the truck driver gave her a blast on his air horn.

"I'll tell you what he's selling, Brady. Good advice. He's a friend of yours and you ought to be thankful for it!"

He made no reply, looking out at the orange groves. The dark green leaves were like wax, the bittersweet smell good to the nose. Aunt Daisy slowed for the cutoff. The small black car dropped down from the highway, trailing a cloud of dust. He could remember the deserted hamlet when forty families had lived there. His first schooling had been in the small frame building now overgrown with weeds. The Communion of Saints had lasted no more than a generation. It had fallen apart from sheer inertia. He'd left it at the age of ten. The military academy in Virginia had been Aunt Daisy's idea. It was her money that put him through U.S.C. Her house had been the only real home he had ever known.

She rolled the Volkswagen into the carport and stalled the motor. Her veined hand covered his.

"I'm glad you're back, Brady. Bring your things in."

He followed her up the steps to the porch. The living room was furnished in a way that had always seemed normal to him. Seeing it after a lapse of time, he realized that a stranger might feel differently. The dresser was old and Welsh but the chairs and table were completely undistinguished. Aunt Daisy had had them sprayed pink at some time. There was a ouija board, a complete set of the works of Madame Blavatsky, several decks of tarot cards. A set of Biblical prints completed the décor. He dropped his bags and went to the porch window. A crate of beer was on the floor out there, next to his aunt's chair. Daisy was no fool.

She'd acquired the post of caretaker through squatter's rights, outlasting the rest of the community by sheer persistence. She'd been paying the state and federal taxes on the property out of her own pocket for the last ten years. Just a little while longer and the entire hamlet would revert to her — seven hundred acres of the best land in the county.

He could hear her in the kitchen, singing in the flat toneless voice that she used when pleased. He let himself into his own room. It was on the south side of the house and caught the sun for most of the day, summer and winter. The bed that had once seemed enormous now left his feet sticking out of the covers. The snapshot on the dresser showed a youngish-looking woman with a 1930 hair style. She was peering into the camera lens with an air of faint embarrassment, as if startled to find herself heavily pregnant. As well she might, he thought. The story was that his parents had gone through a marriage service but no one had ever mentioned his father to him. His mother had died in childbirth.

He started putting his things away in the drawers. He smelled Aunt Daisy's lavender bags with an odd sense of trespassing. He'd grown away from all this — the books by Stevenson and Buchan, the crossed fencing foils on the wall. He had chosen the sport expressly in a football-minded university. He'd learned to fence well if not expertly, enjoying the split-second anticipation more than the need for self-control.

He came back into the living room. Aunt Daisy was in her favorite seat, a wicker-bottomed kitchen chair with four inches sawed off the legs. The alteration allowed her to plant her feet squarely on the ground and at the same time tilt the chair back a little. It was a much-used position. She had taken off her hat. Her long gray hair was loose about her shoulders, a complete contrast to the dark well-defined eyebrows. She rattled an armful of bracelets, pointing at the television set.

"Color. Covers all the channels. I got it yesterday."

The screen was the largest he'd ever seen. One way or another he knew what was coming. "Great," he said.

She nodded as if he had asked her a question. "You're going to be spending a whole lot of time here. You won't want to be playing cards with me all the while. Get the beer."

He smiled because he was very fond of her. "Didn't you hear, Daisy? I'm not supposed to drink."

Her herb cigarette was burning down one side. She took it from her lips and wet the paper with a finger.

"Horse feathers. Beer's not liquor."

There were more bottles in the refrigerator. He emptied a couple into glasses. Like all people who lived alone, Aunt Daisy had certain house rules. She applied them rigorously. If you drank on the porch it was straight from the bottle. Inside the house you were polite. He gave her a glass and sat down. His question was innocent.

"Did Ballantine come for his money?"

She fished a speck of ash from her drink before answering. "He did. I know all about Scott Ballantine, Brady. So does Charley Thornton."

He thought about that for a while. "I didn't imagine you'd be bringing Charley Thornton into our business, Daisy."

"I'm not," she snapped. "Not any more than I can help.

Eighteen hundred dollars! What have you got left — *nothing!* All the money you wasted on that woman!"

He shook his head. "We don't talk about her, remember?"

She sniffed, then her eyes softened suddenly. "Look at yourself in that mirror, boy. You're gray before your time. At your age you shouldn't have a care in the world. But you don't want to talk about the reason for it all. Oh no, not Sir Lancelot!"

He put his glass down carefully. She was wise in spite of her idiosyncrasies — wise and kind, except in one area. Her mind had made a neat package of all his troubles and thrown it into Joanne Kyle's lap. Daisy Palumbo hated even her memory. He changed the subject.

"Did anyone call?" he asked.

She let her chair tilt forward. "Not for you, no."

He knew that she was lying. Ballantine would have kept his promise. The alternative was something Jordan preferred not to think about.

"Come on, sweetheart," he coaxed. "You're the only one I've got. Don't keep hitting me with Charley Thornton, lying to me about telephone calls. I'm not in jail anymore."

Her expression was stubborn. "You're paroled to me and I'm making sure you don't go back."

He grinned at her amiably. "They should have known better. A good-looking girl like you and immoral to boot."

She swung her hand at his behind, her eyes pleased. "You look thin. I'll have to put some good food into you."

He groaned theatrically. "Tuna fish and cranberry jelly. Help."

149

"There's a blue-plate special at the drugstore," she said composedly. "A dollar twenty-five. I thought you could take me into town. They'll be expecting it — that fan club of yours — you might as well get it over."

He pushed her down in her seat. "You listen to me, Daisy. We're going to eat here. As soon as it's dark I've got to get out. I'll need to take your car."

She sat very quiet before looking up at him. "I read those parole papers, Brady. You're not supposed to drive and I'm responsible for you."

"I'm responsible for myself," he argued, "and this is something that I have to do, Daisy."

Tears dribbled from her eyes, streaking the green make-up. He knew her well enough to be sure that the weeping was no sign of weakness. Rage and frustration, more likely.

"It's that woman still, isn't it?" she said in a tight voice.

He nodded. Most of it she'd never understand. Some she did but wouldn't accept.

"You really loved her, didn't you?" Her voice held a hint of longing.

"The only time. She was the only chance I ever had, Daisy. You believe in justice, don't you?"

She coughed on her evil-looking cigarette. "I believe in God's justice. I don't monkey with the rest. God bides his time."

"I can't afford to," he answered. He sat down again so that their knees were touching. "Listen to me, Daisy, I loved Joanne and Kyle killed her. Maybe he didn't do it with his own hands, but he knows who did. Doesn't *any* of

150

this mean anything to you for crissakes?" His voice shook with sudden exasperation.

"You keep a watch on your mouth," his aunt said mechanically. "I tell you justice is for the Almighty. He doesn't need your meddling. Keep out of it."

It was time for the quick, hard chop, without mercy or finesse. It was useless to reason with her. He took the car keys from her purse.

"I'm not going to do anything silly," he promised. "Nobody's going to get hurt. It'll be a simple confrontation. A fact-finding committee of two. Kyle and me. No drama — just the truth."

Her face was woebegone and raddled. "Don't do this to me, Brady."

"I have to, sweetheart. Just this one time. I'll be back tomorrow. I'm not expected at the parole office until Monday. Then if the guy wants me to break rocks, I'll break rocks. I swear it!"

She left the room, slamming the door hard behind her. He went out onto the porch and sat for a while. Creepers swung in the faint breeze. He could hear his aunt banging about in the bedroom. He pictured her, tears streaming down her face. It had been like that, the few times she had ever beaten him as a child. She cried rarely and usually from a sense of despair. She'd come out of it — she always did. One thing was sure. She would protect him from anything and everyone. She was incapable of disloyalty.

He gave her half an hour. Sunshine slanted under the eaves of the porch, falling against her windows. The shades were drawn. He tiptoed down the back steps and crossed

the neighboring yard. The tangle of wild oats and weeds
grew waist high. Cats prowled there, fed by his aunt when-
ever she remembered. He saw one of them now, a thin gray
animal perched in the branches of an apple tree, watching
him. The side door of the schoolhouse was fastened with a
bent nail. He released it and pushed the door open. The
place stank of rat droppings. A pale yellow light filtered
through the filthy windows. He walked between the lines of
old-fashioned desks to a cobwebbed door. It was darker inside. He squatted among the piles of mildewed schoolbooks.
It was a minute or so before he found what he was looking
for. He carried the plastic sack into the long room. Inside
was a .32-caliber automatic. The round ends of the shells
were still bright under a film of grease. He had been working out at Republic, five years before, on an assignment that
had kept him out late. There had been a spate of midnight
muggings. He had bought the gun and obtained a permit
for it. He wiped the weapon off and checked the action. He
stepped outside, wiping the filth from his clothes. He refas-
tened the door with the nail. His contract with Ballantine
would never be fulfilled. The one with Kyle would. It was a
matter of time before the Canadian realied that he'd been
used. That there was going to be no five thousand dollars —
no *dolce vita*. Whatever was left of the eighteen hundred, he
could take. But nobody was going to ask Kyle for money.
He'd denied writing the check in open court and forged
the stub. Once he was confronted with it, he would break.
And when he finally did break, he'd give up whoever had
killed Jo. That was all that Jordan wanted. Meanwhile
the betrayal of Ballantine was an occupational hazard but
one he preferred not to think about.

The light was failing when he backed the Volkswagen out of the carport. Aunt Daisy was still in her room. He saw the curtains move as he drove off. There was nothing he could do there. She'd come out of it the way she always did. It was half-past ten by the time he reached Pacific Ramparts. There was no traffic on the beach road. He maneuvered the Volkswagen in among the trees. The moon threw a latticework of shadow through the branches. The sandy soil was scarred with tire marks. He followed them as far as a dusty Chevrolet sedan hidden well from the road. The doors were unlocked. A can of fish bait lay on the back seat. It could be Ballantine or not.

It was a strange feeling, coming back. He'd closed his eyes a thousand times, smelling the pines, hearing the wash of the ocean — the car starting up on the bluff. He was carrying his jacket. The gun was in the right-hand pocket. He scrambled over a bank of loose sand, approaching the houses from the back. The tide was out. His feet made no sound. A light showed in the Carberry place. The rest of the houses were in darkness. The drive up from Palamos had been too simple. He had never surrendered his driver's license. Daisy's car papers were bundled in a hairnet inside the glove compartment. He'd passed half a dozen Highway Patrol cruisers. The crews had given the small black car no more than cursory inspection. He'd watched them go, feeling nothing. His hunting down of Kyle wouldn't finish that way — he was sure of it. "An act of faith" Ballantine had called it — smiling, of course. The Canadian was high on the smile.

He passed the Kyle house without a sideways glance. The door at the top of the steps of the last porch was open. He

153

stood there silently, looking into the crudely furnished room. There was a map open on the table, a reading lamp next to it, and beyond this a fifth of Scotch and an empty glass. As Jordan moved forward, Ballantine appeared in the doorframe of an inner room. He pointed his finger, cocked his thumb, and grinned.

"Boom-boom, you're dead!"

Jordan found the light switch and put the house in darkness. "It's been a long drive. Fix me a drink."

Ballantine's half-naked body was brown in the pale moonlight. "I heard you coming. A sand flea hops around here and Poppa hears it. I'll get another glass."

He came back from the kitchen, poured the Scotch and added water. "I called your aunt earlier. She said you weren't there."

Jordan kicked off his shoes. A faint breeze was coming off the water. He drained his glass and put it down.

"I wasn't. I got in just before noon. What happened with the sheriff down there?"

Ballantine's chair creaked. "A good question. You should have told me — everyone in Palamos seems to have an interest in Brady Jordan. It was like Old Home Week. The sheriff figured me for some sort of a hoodlum who'd robbed your aunt. It was some time before he gave me the benefit of the doubt."

"Thornton's all right," Jordan told him. "He won't make trouble."

Ballantine's smile was a gleam of teeth in the shadow. "Nobody likes me. Your aunt, the sheriff, and now Tina Kyle."

Anxiety made Jordan's voice abrasive. "Tina Kyle? What have you done there, for crissakes?"

"*Done?*" Ballantine took his chair to the porch. He waited till Jordan followed. "I did what you said — specifically. 'Talk to the girl,' you said. 'Make yourself pleasant,' you said. This is what I got for it." He was holding the top of his lip up.

"Let's have it from the beginning," Jordan said wearily. He listened intently as the other man explained. Getting Ballantine invited into the Kyle house had been an essential part of the scheme. It had never occurred to him that the plan might fail. He looked at Ballantine sourly. "Now what?"

The Canadian's voice was edgy. "You could try singing 'Melancholy Baby'!"

Ballantine had probably used the same aggressive sort of line with the girl. Jordan let it go. "Anything else?" he asked.

Ballantine pointed at the bluff. "I was up there. Everything you said's possible. There are four or five arroyos. A guy could have come down any one of them. So could a woman, come to that."

Jordan scowled. "Don't you start with the theories. The girl was with her father."

"That's right. Everyone was with somebody else." He reached out suddenly, lifting the pocket of Jordan's draped jacket. He cocked his head as he felt its weight. "Something you're going to tell me, Brady?"

Jordan dropped the jacket. "You didn't even see it. You're blind. I know what I'm doing."

Ballantine grimaced. "That's not the point. *I'd* like to know, too."

Jordan's stare was dispassionate. "You're playing hard to get again. I'm getting sick of it, Scott. There's a bus depot seven miles away. I'll drive you there if that's what you want. Only make up your mind and fast. I have things to do."

Their breathing was loud as they measured one another. Ballantine pushed his fingers through his hair. "You're up tighter than a tick, chum. The thing's got you by the balls, hasn't it?" Jordan made no answer. Ballantine continued. "Do you *really* think you know what you're doing?"

"I know," Jordan answered evenly. "And forget about the shooting if that's what's worrying you. There won't *be* any."

"You're damn right it's what's worrying me," Ballantine retorted hotly. "If you want to play cowboy that's your business, but don't involve me. I wouldn't walk a yard with you while you're carrying that thing."

Jordan's hand came up placatingly. "Nobody's going to ask you to. It's late and I'm tired. If you've got any ideas, now's the time to let me hear them."

The Canadian jerked his head at the map. "The social approach is screwed up. I'm going to have to burgle the Kyle place. If the check's there, I'll find it."

Jordan moved his head with conviction. "It's there. You did say 'burgle,' didn't you?"

Ballantine put his hands behind his head. "Burgle. Look, Brady, can't you do any better than 'a loose board in a closet'? She must have said more than that surely."

Jordan had tracked the thought through his memory too

many times not to be sure about the answer. "That's all. Do this any way you want, Scott, just as long as it's done and there are no kickbacks."

Ballantine's eyes crinkled. "Know something — I'm getting a strange feeling about you, Brady, and I'm not too sure that I like it."

Jordan went through the motions of laughing. "What kind of a feeling?"

"A little voice keeps whispering in my ear," said Ballantine. " 'You'd die for Brady but would Brady die for you.' " He was on his feet, grinning in the moonlight.

"You're joking, of course," Jordan said uneasily.

Ballantine nodded. "Of course."

The conversation had taken a turn that was making Jordan uneasy. He changed the subject.

"I've left Daisy's car in the pines. I'd better put it out of sight. There'll be people here over the weekend."

The Canadian gathered the empty glasses. "I'll take care of it. That house on the bluff is empty. I'll put it in the cypresses out of sight. Nobody goes there." He held out his hand.

Jordan gave him the car keys. "I'm staying till Sunday night. Daisy will cover for me."

The wind banged the porch door. Ballantine jerked his head toward the bedroom.

"Help yourself. Mine's the one near the window. I'll be right back."

Jordan heard the Volkswagen being driven up on the headland. He was feigning sleep when the other man returned.

Sebastian G. Kyle   June 1970

HE HAD BEEN SITTING in the study for almost two hours now. Tina had eaten little at dinner. Shortly afterward she'd excused herself from the backgammon board and gone up to her room pleading a headache. He could see her bedroom windows from where he was sitting. Her lights had been turned out for some time. He laid his spectacles on top of the tape recorder and thumbed the playback button. His monologue was disjointed — comments on the script he had been reading. He heard his voice falter as he made an observation about the trial scene. He stopped the machine, unwilling to endure it any longer. Hundreds of thousands of dollars and some of the best brains in the business were being employed to produce a macabre hoax: a hoax that he could explode with a few short words.

He'd carried the secret around for over a year, a Pandora's box that he opened, impelled by some morbid desire to relive the past. Tina was right. Joanne's revenge was at work on him even now. Memory shaped her presence in the glass, standing behind him as he shaved. Her voice called his name in broad daylight, mocking him. For the first time in his existence he was taking barbiturates in order to sleep. Worst of all was the barrier that Joanne's spirit was building between Tina and himself. His daughter was the only thing he had left. She'd be lost unless he managed to smash his way through to her. Somehow he had to find the courage to tell her the truth.

He switched off the study lights and checked the house.
Mrs. Bruce had gone to bed. The dog was upstairs with
Tina. He went outside. The still surface of the pool reflected points of light nailed to the indigo sky. He'd known
what he had to do ever since Tina had told him about the
stranger on the beach. He had to go and see for himself.

He backed the Rolls out of the garage. The old car had
over a hundred thousand miles on the speedometer but the
motor was still soundless. He drove through the thicket using his parking lights, turning on the heads when he reached
the highway. The trip down the valley took him twenty
minutes. Pacific Ramparts was still lively. The main street
was crowded with out-of-town cars. The Community Center
Theater was doing good business. He drove on, taking the
road to Las Rosas. A short distance out, he forked west on
the cutoff, climbing the spine of the northern bluff. He cut
his lights and stopped at the padlocked chain across the way.
Sy Harris had been in Europe for three years now. Kyle
thought about it with sudden longing. He lit a thin cheroot,
looking down at the beach. An oily turquoise sea washed
the sand like oatmeal. The houses below were in darkness.
He imagined the stranger sitting in the Carberry place. Kyle
moved out of sight wearily. His courage was gone. He
needed some of Tina's youth and defiance. But to tap her
strength he had to tell her the truth. There could no longer
be any question of sparing himself. She had to know everything — the agony, rage, and humiliation. And she had to
know about his love. No matter how much it hurt her, she
had to accept his love for Joanne.

He went back in time to the night when it had all started
— or finished. It didn't make much difference. His "good

thing," as the kids said, had ended. He'd been outside, sitting in the swing by the pool. It was late afternoon. Tina was riding horseback somewhere or other. Mrs. Bruce was in the house. He heard the sound of Joanne's car long before it turned off the highway. She came through the trees driving dangerously fast and skidded off the gravel into the garage. He heard the door of her convertible slammed. Seconds later, she was coming across the grass. She changed direction, seeing him and came over, taking off her driving gloves. He remembered how her hair had looked in the sunlight, her tanned arms and legs. The blue dress that she'd been wearing molded the firmness of her breasts. She sat down beside him and pushed the hair from her eyes. For once she was smiling.

"Why the face, sweetie pie?" she asked. "I thought you'd be pleased to see me."

The swim had left him exhausted. He covered his flabby stomach with a towel self-consciously. "I'm always pleased to see you, dear. I only wish it were more often."

She swung a bare leg, still looking at him and smiling. "Now there's a cute thing for a girl to hear!"

He sensed the mockery in her tone. "It's been a good day, Joanne. Don't let's spoil it, please."

"I'm spoiling nothing." She spoke with offhand contempt. "How about you, though, with the Roscoe Agency?"

He bent down, hiding his face under the pretext of finding his spectacles. He'd been ultracareful in his choice of detective agency. A call to the Chamber of Commerce had given the address of the Roscoe people. He could only think that someone there had sold him out.

"I'm human, Joanne," he said reasonably. "These months

have been agony for me. I had to know the truth. You're playing with two people's lives, remember."

Her eyes taunted him. "You must be talking about you and your daughter. I've never understood what you wanted a wife for. You had such a sweet thing going with Tina. Don't think I haven't had my doubts about the pair of you."

The words were like a whip across his face. "You must be really evil to say a thing like that."

She hiked her skirt up over bare brown thighs. "I wonder what other people would say. Setting your wife up in a divorce action — actually *hiring* a lover! Don't you think that's evil?"

He tried to take her arm unsuccessfully. "It's still not too late, Joanne. I've never stopped loving you. We can leave here tonight, go away somewhere together."

Her mouth thinned with distaste. "If you ever lay a hand on me again," she said coldly, "you'll regret it as long as you live. I'll tell you something else, Sebastian. Take it to bed with you tonight. I'm leaving you for Brady Jordan. Permanently. I'm going to see Liebowitz tomorrow. What you've done to me is going to cost you money."

Leaving him for Jordan. The twist was ironical. She gave him little enough time to think about it.

"Don't take it to heart, lover. You've still got Tina."

He sat there alone for a long time after she had gone into the house, deflated, ashamed, and hopeless. It was six o'clock when he followed her in. He heard Tina's horse kicking in its box stall. He went upstairs quickly, not wanting to face her. One wife had run rather than share his life. The second was on her way unless he moved quickly. The first thing he

162

had to do was call off the agency. He used the phone in his bedroom. The line clicked open. A recorded voice cut in before Kyle could speak.

"This is the Roscoe Detective Agency downtown in the heart of Los Angeles. This recording is an emergency measure due to unforeseen circumstances. Mr. Roscoe will attend to your inquiry personally as soon as he returns. Please state your message clearly, starting *now!*"

He replaced the receiver. A bathroom separated his room from his wife's. He tried the doorknob on her side. It was locked. There was no answer to his soft rapping. He called the agency five times before dinner. The same recorded voice replied. The meal was purgatory. The two women were icily polite to one another, shafting their arrows through him. Joanne could be merciless on this sort of occasion. He waited for her to make the public announcement that she was leaving him. For some reason it never came. Mrs. Bruce brought coffee. Joanne refused it, looking at her watch ostentatiously.

"It's such a wonderful night — I think I'll drive over to the beach. I might even sleep there."

She was smiling across the table at him. He followed her out into the hall. "Don't go," he asked in a low voice. "The detectives are going to be there. They're taking photographs."

She was swinging her car keys from her forefinger. "You wouldn't dare. Anyway, you're forgetting something — I'll have Brady to take care of me."

Her careless defiance challenged him to do his worst. She picked up her purse from the table and pushed past

163

him. He was still standing, looking out the front door, when Tina came from the dining room. She was plain beside Joanne's patrician elegance.

"What was all that about?" she demanded.

He turned away but too late. She was at his side in a second, brushing the tears from his cheeks with furious fingers.

"Don't *do* it! Don't you *dare* cry — that bitch isn't worth it!"

He managed to control himself. "Leave me alone. I *have* to be alone, Tina."

Her touch lingered on his face for a moment. Then she turned and walked the length of the house. He heard her switch on the television set. It was Friday night. A two-hour drama was showing on one of the channels. He knew that she would watch it. He gave her a little time to settle down, locked the study door on the inside, and left through the French windows. Half an hour took him to the beach. He had left the car where he was sitting now, high on the bluff. Instinct — cunning? He'd never worked it out. He scrambled down the arroyo. Lights were showing in the beach house. He could hear the sound of the record player. He climbed the steps to the porch, recognizing the acrid odor of marijuana. That she used it meant nothing to him. There was no crime that he would not have shared with her willingly at that moment.

She must have heard him arrive and came running from the bedroom, one hand flying to her hair. She was wearing a pair of silk lounging pajamas. It was obvious that was all she was wearing. Her welcoming smile faded.

"My God, not *you* again!"

Her expression changed to fear as he came forward. She turned and ran for the bedroom. He managed to get a foot in the door and hold it open. The bedside lamp was burning. The sheets had been turned down, ready for occupation. His voice was that of a stranger.

"It'll be the way you want, Joanne — any way at all from now on. I need you. Don't leave me."

She was between the wall and the bed. She fired the answer at him like a bullet. "You don't even have any dignity left — *nothing!* You make me physically sick, do you understand. Sick — sick — *sick!*"

He slapped her hard with his open hand. She staggered, hitting her head against the wall. She fell on her back on the bed. As he leaned forward, she spat full in his face. His fingers found her neck. He closed his eyes firmly, increasing the pressure, trying to avoid her raking nails. She fought like a weasel, a low gurgling sound in her throat. When he opened his eyes again, she was lying quite still. A mask of foam covered her nose and mouth. He hurried away, the sound of the record player following him along the beach. Fear gave him speed and strength to climb the arroyo. He drove home fast, making a detour to avoid the town. The clock in the study was chiming as he came through the French windows. He had been absent from the house for one hour and twenty-five minutes. He unlocked the corridor door. Tina was still in the drawing room. He could see the back of her head. He went up to the bathroom and washed. There was blood on his hands. Nails had raked through his shirt in half a dozen places. He changed the shirt and went downstairs again.

Tina was curled on the couch. She made room for him beside her. He nodded at the screen. "Is it any good? I thought I heard you laugh."

She made a face. "It must have been in despair. There's this girl who keeps getting pregnant. They don't seem to have heard of the Pill in Yugoslavia. Are you feeling any better, darling?"

"Much." He stretched cautiously, feeling a pain in his shoulder. Joanne must have bitten him during the struggle. Something impelled him to add, "I hope Joanne doesn't decide to sleep at the beach. She shouldn't be out there on her own."

His daughter's eyes sought his. "Say it aloud, Father. 'She won't *be* there alone.' Say it out loud!"

His head dropped. His voice was dull. "I can't." It was half an hour later when the phone rang. Mrs. Bruce had taken the call. Sheriff Kowalsky was on the line.

He broke the chain of memories with an effort. A light came and went in the Carberry house. A figure moved in the darkness. Someone was standing on the front porch. For a moment he thought that he recognized Jordan. It had to be a trick of light. He climbed back into the Rolls. Joanne was dead. Tomorrow he would tell his daughter how and why. The ghost would be laid to rest for once and all. Oak Valley stood silent in the moonlight, the shadows around it sharply etched. He closed the French windows behind him and secured the house. Above all he needed sleep. Tomorrow's session at the studio promised to be a tough one. He was still fighting for the right to control the final cut. It was a losing battle but pride forced him to continue. He switched on a lamp and scribbled a note for his daughter.

Stay away from the beach, darling. There's no real reason why — it's just a feeling. I'll try to be home early. I want to talk to you.

He started up the stairs. A strip light illuminated the portrait of his first wife. The artist had painted her in a moment of flight. Her great startled eyes seemed to follow him as he passed. He flipped the master switch at the head of the stairs, extinguishing all the lights below. The wide corridor duplicated that beneath, running the length of the house. The dove gray carpet was a shade lighter than the walls. He slipped the note under Tina's door. She had been in his room. His bed was turned down. A small glass of brandy was on the table, a substitute for the sleeping pills that she hated him to take. He emptied the glass in the bathroom and swallowed a couple of barbiturate tablets. There was no point in her knowing that he did the same, night after night. He hid the vial at the back of the medicine chest.

The bathroom was carpeted. A pale green tub was sunk in the floor and the fittings were feminine. There was a make-up table with angle mirrors. Dryads sported on the tiles. He opened the door to what had once been Joanne's room. Tina had stripped it of every trace of his wife. Her clothes had been given to the Goodwill. Many things Tina had simply burned. The bed was unmade. The fitted closet stood open, showing rows of empty hangers.

167

He had made no protest then or since. He recognized his daughter's need to destroy every memory of a woman she had hated. The funeral service had been grotesque. It was held in a salt mist blowing in from the coast. The minister had a cold. Tina had stood close to him. She'd refused to wear black. Her behavior had scandalized some, bewildered others. She personally had remained glacially indifferent.

He shut the door again, washed, and prepared for bed. He fell asleep quickly, the light by his side still burning.

Scott Ballantine   June 1970

HE WAS SITTING propped in the fork of an oak tree. He had left the Chevrolet a mile away, hidden in the orange grove. He was wearing his sneakers, a dark shirt, and trousers. The bag hanging around his neck contained the tools he had brought with him. A small crowbar, piece of mica, and a wood chisel. He'd bought each article at a different hardware store, explaining its need at length with an odd feeling that the salesclerks were on to him. The crude burglar's kit was a far cry from the specially made instruments that the Texan had described: forceps for turning keys from the outside of a lock, slivers of steel that could probe tumblers and lift them, collapsible ladders made of aluminum that would hook onto a window ledge or gutter. He remembered the oil-derrick drawl. *The night's your friend, pardner. You're the invisible man — God!*

At the moment he felt a long way from either. His eyes strained, peering into the darkness till imagination peopled the shadows with moving figures. There were no lights in the house. He'd approached the woods from the back, coming around from the stables. That had been his first bad moment. The stallion kicked out suddenly, a hoof thudding against the door of the stall. The noise had caught Ballantine halfway across the yard, treading like a man walking on eggs. He'd lurched and fallen. The stallion's head appeared above the door, ears pricked as it located him. He picked himself up to the sound of the animal's whinny. He checked the garage. The Rolls was out, the girl's station wagon in its usual place. There was no sign of the dog. He moved quickly into the oak copse. The confidence he'd displayed for Jordan was leaking by the minute. He chose a tree where he could see the whole front of the house and hauled himself into the branches. An hour or so went by before he heard a car turning in off the highway. The Rolls passed immediately beneath him, Kyle alone at the wheel. Seconds later the soft putt-putt of the exhaust was silenced. Ballantine took a new grip and leaned out to get a better view. Something small and ferocious was crawling on his neck, biting. Probably red ants. He dared not move. Kyle was walking around the pool toward the study. His white dinner jacket located him deep into the shadow. The French windows were dragged open. A light came on in the study. He could see Kyle at the desk, writing. The lamp was extinguished. New lights replaced it, this time upstairs. If Jordan was right they located Kyle's room, and his daughter slept opposite. The bugs bit. He grew stiffer. Kyle's light still burned. His watch showed ten past two. He let himself drop from the tree, landing on ferns. Everyone in the house slept at the east end. The housekeeper's quarters were directly beneath the girl's bedroom. If he didn't hit the place now, he knew he never would.

He flitted through the trees to the far end of the house. He left the bag of tools in the end of a storm drain. The thought of splintering glass and tearing wood was suddenly repugnant. He had never claimed to be a Raffles. He pulled on a pair of skin gloves and tried the nearest window. It was locked vertically and horizontally by bolts. A second and third window were fastened in the same way. The frames rattled and his breathing was loud. Daytime suddenly seemed a much better bet. He was on his way back to the cover of the trees when he noticed the roof over on the west wing. It was flat. A stone stairway led to it from the back of the house. His feet made no sound in the sneakers. There was a sun-bathing mattress behind a small parapet. The roof was obviously used. He craned over the edge. A window ledge jutted out beneath. He saw the fold of a curtain flutter. He stretched himself out, lying over the parapet on his stomach. He grabbed the brickwork and lowered himself gingerly till his feet touched the sill. He crouched there for a moment then jackknifed through the open space. It was completely dark inside. He stood still to get his bearings. He could hear water trickling and the smell in his nostrils was surely soap. His eyes focused gradually. He was in what had to be a guest bathroom at the back of the house. He held his breath, inching the door ajar. A slit of light at the end of the corridor located Kyle's bedroom. The feeling of fear was gone. He suddenly knew what the Texan had meant — the invisible man. He was inside the house and nobody knew it. It was an oddly exciting sensation. He tiptoed down the corridor, keeping close to the wall. He passed a staircase on his left and bent at the keyhole of Kyle's door. The aperture offered a foreshortened view of the bed. Kyle was sitting upright, propped by pillows, fast asleep. His teeth were in a glass by his side and he was breathing heavily.

Ballantine moved to the right, remembering what Jordan had said. This would be the dead woman's bedroom. He went behind the opening door silently. As he closed it a dog barked. He looked around frantically for a hiding place. An open clothes closet extended the width of the room. He stepped into darkness smelling of camphor. Someone was moving out in the corridor. He heard the door open. Then the light came on. The hammering in his chest seemed to fill the closet. The girl's reflection showed in the mirror. Her face was greasy and she was wearing pajamas. She was holding the terrier in her arms. All she had to do was glance left and he was discovered. She bent down, lifting the bed cover so that the dog could see beneath.

"See for yourself," she scolded. "There's nothing there, stupid." The dog continued to whine.

Then the light was extinguished. It was minutes before he could bring himself to leave the shelter of the closet. He tiptoed toward the bathroom and heard Kyle's heavy breathing. It was past three. All he wanted to do was to get out of there as quickly as he could. The closet floor was made of solid parquet. There was no chance of anything being hidden beneath it. He looked down from the window. The drop was easy but it would mean leaving the window open. It was shut now. He pulled the corridor door open in stages. He eased himself out, watching the door opposite. The loud ticking of a clock funneled up from the hallway. Three quick steps took him to the head of the stairs. Ten more and he was standing in the hallway itself. There was enough light to see the jockey cap and whip on a chair. The rooms at both ends of the corridor were open. His ears were on stalks, listening for a sound from upstairs. None came. The front door was secured by two locks. The heavy mortise was not in use. He turned the catch of the spring lock and stepped outside. A one-eared cat stalked from under a bush, its tail lashing. He bent down swiftly and grabbed the animal by the neck. It hung limply in his hand. He tossed it into the hallway and closed the door quietly. If Kyle's daughter still had doubts about the nocturnal disturbance, this should put her mind at rest.

The road back to Pacific Ramparts was deserted. Lamps shone on rows of garbage cans ready for collection. A car was parked out in front of the one sad diner. He left the Chevrolet in the trees. The sky had lightened to a Wedgwood blue. The surf was breaking far out. He had left the bag of tools in his haste. No matter, he'd need them again. The porch steps creaked as he climbed them. Jordan was still up, sitting on a chair outside. The floor was littered with butts. His naked chest shone with sweat.

"You've been a helluva time." He said it as if he were committing the fact to memory.

Ballantine kicked his shoes and trousers off. He balled his shirt and threw it at the end of the porch. The air was good on his skin. He went into the kitchen and poured a beer. He dropped into the vacant chair. "I don't know that I like your tone any too much. I *know* what time it is. You've been sitting on your can and I've been working."

"Great." There was a hint of sarcasm in Jordan's voice.

Ballantine tilted his head back and drank. "Kyle didn't get back till well after midnight. The other two were already in bed when I got there."

173

"He was here," said Jordan. "Up on the bluff. Watching this place."

Ballantine produced his own surprise. "There's nothing in Joanne's closet. The floor's solid."

Jordan's voice was incredulous. "You mean you've actually been inside the house?"

"For the best part of an hour." The Canadian grinned.

Jordan leaned forward. "I know the layout of that house. If you were in Joanne's room there were only two doors between you and Kyle."

"And the girl sleeps across the corridor," Ballantine said equably. "There's a dog and a cat and Kyle snores. Do you want me to go on?"

Jordan moved in the twilight. He lit a cigarette and waited.

"The dog was sleeping in the girl's room. I guess it must have heard me. Anyway, the Kyle girl picked it up as she came into Joanne's bedroom. I could have reached out and touched her. I was standing in the closet."

"And she didn't see you?" The question was only just short of open disbelief.

"She didn't know I was there," Ballantine said simply.

Jordan's cigarette seemed to have lost its flavor. The butt spiraled into the darkness. He went through the motions of applauding.

"Thank you, Jimmy Valentine."

"You're a strange guy," said Ballantine. "There isn't a man in the world who could have done better than I did tonight and what happens — you want to give me a hard time. I'm going back there tomorrow. I know the house now. It'll be easy."

Jordan accompanied him to his feet. "You want me to come with you — to the Kyle place I mean?"

The thought made Ballantine uneasy. "Hell, no. Stay here and pray."

He opened all the doors and windows to get as much air into the place as possible. Jordan was already in bed.

Ballantine awoke suddenly, the dream persisting into his consciousness. The vivid scene had been a re-creation of his arrival at state prison. A file of cons dragged their feet across the flood-lit yard to the catcalls from the cellblocks. He lay quite still, contemplating the shabby room. The homemade chairs, the out-of-date fisherman's catalog reassured him of reality. Jordan's bed was made, the blankets neatly folded.

Ballantine rolled sideways and found the floor with his feet. The sun was high beyond the open window. It was almost eleven o'clock. A man was putting up a tent at the far end of the beach. He could hear the kids with him shouting. He went into the shower and shocked himself into consciousness with cold water. Jordan was in the kitchen already dressed and shaved. The table had been set for one. The ham and eggs must have been cooked while Ballantine was showering. Jordan filled a cup with coffee and pushed it over. Ballantine sat down, wrapping the damp towel around his loins. The food was hot and he went at it hungrily. Jordan dropped the dirty dishes in the sink and sat opposite Ballantine.

"You were talking in your sleep."

Ballantine struck a match to a cigarette. He let the first exhalation go with satisfaction.

"So were you. We ought to exchange confidences."

175

Jordan frowned. "You're still sure you don't want me to come over there with you? It might be better if you get rid of the check as soon as possible."

"You're going to stay right here," Ballantine ordered. "And keep out of sight. There are people at the other end of the beach."

Jordan looked out across the pools left in the rippled sand. "You don't have to worry about me."

Ballantine was on his way to the bedroom. "But I do," he said pointedly. "That's our hang-up now. We've started to worry about one another."

He shaved and dressed, putting on a clean shirt, tan slacks, and the sneakers. He made sure that his identification papers were with him. He'd learned that much by experience. He was about to leave when he remembered the gun. He looked under Jordan's pillow. Nothing. Instinct alone made him turn. Jordan's approach from the kitchen had been silent. He leaned against the side of the door, his green eyes narrowed.

"Was there something you wanted?"

"The gun," said Ballantine. "You'd better let me take it."

Jordan ignored the outstretched hand, his smile bland. "What gun, kid? You're imagining things, old buddy."

Ballantine shook his head. "I never saw you like this before, Brady. What the hell's getting into you?"

Jordan's face was impassive. "Let's talk about you. As I understand it, you're proposing to walk into this house in broad daylight. And what happens if somebody sees you?"

Ballantine combed his hair in the glass. "Nobody's going to see me. I shall flit like a wraith, if that's the word. Straight to your loose floorboard. I know where it is."

The news startled Jordan out of his pose. "How do you mean you *know?*"

Ballantine played the card flamboyantly. "You say she'd hidden things before — things she didn't want Kyle to find, right? Where better than in his daughter's room? It's one place he'd never have thought of looking."

There was no doubt now of Jordan's interest. "Now you're really talking! It's the sort of thing Jo would have gotten a kick out of doing."

"And that's where it'll be." Ballantine's assurance was absolute — the split-second certainty that hits a gambler as the card crosses the table.

He cut himself sandwiches in the kitchen and took a bottle of beer. Jordan came as far as the front porch with him.

"You might see other things of value. Don't touch a thing. The check's what we're interested in. Everything rides on that check, remember."

"*You* remember," said Ballantine. "I'm not likely to forget." It was past noon. The people at the far end of the beach were building a barbecue pit. The Kyle place was empty. Thought of seeing the girl provoked him in a strange way. Even stranger was the thought that his hostility for her was almost forgotten.

Pacific Ramparts was gay with flags. A ball game was going out at Fairfax Park. He pulled to one side, letting the high school band blow its way past. Slim-thighed drum majorettes strutted across the intersection and vanished. He wheeled the Chevrolet through the back streets and onto Route 28. Half an hour later he stopped, deep in the orange grove. The oranges had long since been harvested and the grove was remote, a mile or so away from Oak Valley. His shirt was already plastered to his back. He crossed the road, approaching the oak thicket from the west. It was cooler once he was into the trees. Ten minutes took him to a point where he could see the long rambling house. Someone was running a vacuum cleaner in the hallway. He worked his way around toward the sound. Heavy foliage broke the sunlight over the ferns. His nighttime visit seemed to have gone unremarked. All the doors and windows were open. He could see the gray-haired woman in the hallway now. No sign of Kyle or the girl. The Rolls was out. He found the storm drain and took the wood chisel from his bag. The flat roof over the west wing looked a whole lot lower than it had a few hours ago.

It was four o'clock when he heard the noise of hooves on the graveled driveway. He ducked well back into cover. Tina Kyle jogged by, the terrier panting along behind, inches of tongue showing. The stallion's flanks were soaked. Its rider looked equally exhausted. Her hair was bound in a scarf. Her face was shiny with sweat. Half an hour went by and she came out of the stables. He heard her voice inside the house calling to the older woman. Sound carried distinctly across the pool. He might have been fifteen yards away instead of fifty. Tina Kyle came through the study windows, wearing a canary-colored bikini. She climbed onto the high board. Brown limbs flashed and she hit the water with clean economy. A rhythmic splashing pinpointed her progress. She swam four lengths, hauled herself out, and stretched on the swing seat. The housekeeper brought a tray of food. As far as he could see, the girl barely touched it. His premonition looked like it was coming true. He was in for a long wait. It was half-past four. A small stream ran through the copse, joining a creek beyond the paddock. The stream was no more than a yard wide but blissfully cool. He took off his sneakers and sat with his feet in the water. The sandwiches were inedible. Jordan must have used the knife on soap. He drank the beer, planning his move. It was no trick to work his way around to the west wing. There were half a dozen open windows there. A swift dash across the gravel would put him through one of them. He delayed the assault deliberately. Maybe the housekeeper was upstairs. The girl might want something from her room. He swung his feet out of the water, Jordan on his mind. For nine months they'd been close in the way men in jail come to be. Yet he'd only once seen Jordan show real feeling. Most of the time he spoke of the dead woman's past affairs with surprising tolerance. He'd been describing her body as he found it that night. His eyes were cold and merciless. The lapse had been quickly covered but not before Ballantine had registered it. Now Jordan had a gun.

Ballantine put his shoes on hurriedly. A car was coming along the driveway. He recognized the sound of the Rolls, a heavy swish on gravel. By the time he reached his vantage point Kyle was walking over the grass toward the pool. He was wearing dark gray flannel pants and an alpaca jacket. He moved his legs as if he were tired. Tina Kyle called across the pool. The terrier ran to greet her father.

"Why didn't you take my call at the studio?"

Kyle sat down beside her. Their voices carried plainly at this distance.

"I didn't want to talk there. I told you in the note. I'd be home early."

Ballantine had come as far as he dared. Tina had changed her bikini for an apple green shirt and slacks. She groped under her seat for matches and her cigarettes.

"But that's exactly why I called," he heard her say. "I didn't understand your message. I was worried."

Kyle rose, putting his fingers on her lips. His head signified the open French windows behind him. He pulled her to her feet. They walked toward a door in the wall between the pool and the garage. Kyle unfastened it. Ballantine had a glimpse of color — of bushes fat with roses. He followed them on impulse, running around the pool to the garden wall. The angles of the buildings hid him from anyone in the house. No more than a double course of bricks separated him from the couple sitting in the rose garden. It was Kyle who was doing the talking. The quiet British voice was unfaltering to the end. He might have been describing the changing of the guard instead of his wife's murder. His confession was detailed and explicit. There was a long silence. Then the girl's self-control went. Ballantine could hear her sobbing, her father's efforts to soothe her.

He tiptoed away soundlessly. Murder had always been something you read about — the killer and victims no more than names culled from a crime report. This was different and somehow shocking. He ran back to his vantage point. The shades were drawn on the sunny side of the study. He made up his mind, emboldened by the knowledge of Kyle's guilt. He wiped his feet carefully. His sneakers had tracked wet from the swimming pool. The room was chintz and sunshine with pictures of horses on the wall. He could see the housekeeper sitting in a yard at the back, the one-eared cat in her lap. He navigated the corridor, moving on the balls of his feet, went up the staircase unhurriedly.

Tina Kyle's bedroom door was open. Underclothes were strewn everywhere. A couple of framed photographs stood on the dressing table. One was of Kyle. The other was of the woman whose portrait hung on the staircase. He edged near the window, keeping himself flat against the wall. The housekeeper's chair was directly underneath. He could hear her talking to the cat. A couple of walls and fifty yards were between her and the pair in the rose garden. But Ballantine had a clear view of them. Kyle was sitting bolt upright, his daughter's head cradled in his arms.

Ballantine turned away. The room was fragrant and feminine. The sort of room he had almost forgotten. A toy bear lay across the pillows, battered and chewed. The toy, the disarray of clothing suggested defenseless femininity. The impression rebutted everything he had decided about her. He pulled the wood chisel from his pocket. The door to the clothes closet had been left dragged back on its rollers. He knelt down, pushing his head in among the hanging dresses. He felt among the rows of shoes. The bottom of the closet was lined with hardboard. Obviously it predated the one in Mrs. Kyle's room. He eased up the edge of a board with the chisel and groped beneath. His fingers touched something among the shavings. He pulled out a dusty enve-.lope and replaced the lining. The envelope still smelled faintly of a woman's scent. He extracted the blue slip of paper. Kyle's one mistake was boldly inscribed: *Pay Brady Jordan* $375⁰⁰⁄₁₀₀. The signature was firm and legible.

A door creaked outside in the garden. Ballantine reached the window in time to see Kyle and his daughter walking arm in arm to the garage. His mind raced ahead, seeking the reason for their sudden departure. The secret they shared made them outlaws — put them beyond the comfort or counsel of friends. Other than one another they had nothing and nobody. He craned to see farther out of the window. The housekeeper was still in her chair, an open newspaper across her knees. He put the check in his pocket and raced downstairs. The Rolls was gliding through the thicket. He heard the horn sounded at the junction. He was on his way out of the study when a thought struck him. He went back to the desk. Easy enough to imagine the scene as it had been on the night of Jordan's arrest. The deputies standing here, shuffling their feet, certain that they had the right man locked up in town. After the fruit-less search of the bedroom Kyle himself had suggested that they search his desk. It had been Kyle who volunteered his checkbooks for inspection. He knew what he was doing — knew that the only entry that mattered had been forged. His bank statement would have told him that the check had never been presented for payment. He'd figure that

Jordan couldn't have it or it would have been produced at the trial. The logical conclusion was that it had been lost. Kyle's oath that he'd paid Jordan no money had been made confidently. This check proved him a liar. The forged stub would damn him completely.

Ballantine wiped his face on his sleeve. The middle drawer in the desk was locked. He used the chisel on it and flipped through the papers inside. There were three old checkbooks near the bottom. Apparently the Englishman's habit was to tear across the covers, keeping no more than the stubs themselves as records. The documents in Ballantine's hands were useless. None dated back further than the previous December. Added to that, Kyle had changed his bank.

He swung to face the noise, sensing the presence behind him. Tina Kyle came through the French windows. She must have approached the house while his back was to her. He pushed the splintered drawer back slowly. Her eyes were swollen but they showed no fear. She moved with startling speed, streaking for the phone on the desk. He beat her to it, trapping her wrists.

"I wouldn't," he warned. He let her go, holding the check so that she could read it.

Something seemed to have happened to her voice. "What are you doing here?"

He put the check back in his pocket. Her expression told him that she understood its meaning only too well.

"Where's your father gone?" he asked harshly.

She put her hand to her mouth uncertainly. "He didn't say. Just that he had to go somewhere."

183

She was obviously shaken — too shaken to lie. He pointed at the sofa. She crossed the room obediently and sat down, her knees close together.

"Now you listen to me," he said. "And get this into your head. I've been here since one o'clock. I saw your father arrive. I *know* who killed Joanne. Get it?"

She did the best with what she had, looking up at him defiantly. "I don't know what you're talking about."

"You know," he insisted. "I was on the other side of that wall."

Her hands were trembling. "They won't believe you. It's your word against ours."

"You're forgetting the check," he reminded her.

Her eyes sought his miserably. "What do you want with my father — what are you going to do to him?"

"See that he keeps a contract. He made it."

Her voice was suddenly bitter with accusation. "You're an extortionist. I should have known it. You're in this with Jordan. He sent you here."

Somebody knocked on the door. The housekeeper's voice sounded uncertainly. "Is that you, Miss Tina?"

She signaled him to move behind the door. She opened it a couple of inches.

"It's all right, Mrs. Bruce. It's someone from the riding club." She closed the door firmly and the footsteps retreated.

Tina Kyle's words came in a rush. "If it's money we can give you more than he can."

It was the sort of proposition you'd be justified in putting to an extortionist. He missed nothing of her calculation. He was seeing himself for the first time as she saw him.

"I'll let that one go," he said wearily.

She looked him full in the face, lips parted. "It needn't be just the money; I love my father more than anything else in the world. There's nothing I wouldn't do for him. *Nothing*," she repeated meaningly.

His eyes lingered on her throat. The skin there was lighter than the rest, the color of a ripening apricot. A perverse wish to wound prompted his answer.

"There's nothing you've got that I want."

She flinched as though he had struck her. "I deserved that. I'm sorry. It was a cheap trick." Something in his face seemed to encourage her. She pleaded. "*Please* listen to me."

The agony in her voice left him no choice. "It won't make any difference," he warned.

She took a long deep breath, putting her hands behind her. "There are some people who are completely evil — you must know that. People who destroy everything that they touch. My stepmother was like that. Nothing was sacred to her. My father didn't just love her — he *needed* her. Needed her the way you and I need to breathe. She was young and beautiful and elegant, and as long as she was his he would never grow old." She stopped to gauge the effect of her plea.

He lit a cigarette. "He killed her, didn't he?"

She shook her head desperately. "I don't know how much you heard this afternoon but *I'll* tell you something about that last night. I lived it. That woman took my father's love — she took his misery and spat it back in his face. Don't you *see* what that could do to a sensitive man? There wasn't one single person from her past at the funeral. No friend or lover — nobody. I'm telling you that she was a woman who *had* to die violently. If it hadn't been my father it would have been someone else."

"I know someone who mourned her," he reminded. "Still does. Only he never got to go to the funeral. Your father made sure of that."

Her hands came from behind her, reaching out to him. "Nothing will change the past. I'm asking for his future and mine. Whatever money you want, you'll get. I swear it. But I beg you to have pity on me."

He shifted uncomfortably, moved in spite of himself. "How much pity have you ever given?"

She was standing by the desk. She went on her knees slowly, tears streaming down her face.

"None. I know it. But look at me if you can. I'm pleading for an old man's life. A man who is gentle and good. Help me!"

He glanced away rather than show her that she had failed. She moved in the second, her hand streaking for a side drawer in the desk. She scrambled up, holding a heavy service revolver. She aimed the barrel at him, sobbing.

"Give me the check."

A cold hand crept into his chest and held his heart tight for a moment. All she had to do was pull the trigger and reach for the phone. The only evidence against her father had been destroyed. He was a prowler she had caught in the house. They wouldn't even bring a charge against her. He stepped forward, steeling himself.

"I don't believe you can — not even for him. I'm flesh and blood the same as you are."

The barrel wavered as he neared her. He made no attempt to take the weapon from her. He felt its hardness against his heart. Then the gun clattered to the ground. She put her hands behind her again like a small girl caught stealing. She seemed on the point of saying something. He turned and ran for the trees. He drove out of the orange grove, still shocked and disturbed. Six miles out of Pacific Ramparts he saw the Rolls approaching. He had a brief compulsion to swing the Chevrolet across the highway, to force Kyle to stop. But for what? To hand him over to the justice he himself had always denied? He kept going, passing the stately black limousine without a sideways glance. He was thinking of the girl now, not the father. An agony he had never known had forced her to her knees — despair had pushed the gun into her hand. One quick squeeze of the trigger would have saved her father. But she'd failed him and the memory would stay with her forever.

He parked in front of the Ramparts Hotel. He walked into a bar and grill across the street. The only person there was the Mexican barman. Ballantine ordered a drink and took it to a booth. He pulled the check from his pocket and smoothed it out in front of him. Odd that a small piece of paper should hold the power of life and death. He sat there for almost an hour, the drink untouched, trying to make up his mind. He reached the decision resignedly, as if he had known all along what he would do. Pity was part of love and that much he could find for her. That the rest would never be added made no difference. He paid his bill.

The picnickers' car had gone. Their barbecue pit had been left to the incoming tide. The heat of the day lingered in a shimmering bank above the sand. The breeze had given up. Even up on the bluff, the branches of the cypresses were still. He approached the house from the back. The kitchen door was locked. He walked around the porch to the front. The screen door was on the hook. He unfastened it, looking around curiously. Jordan seemed to have spent his time cleaning house. The dishes had been washed and stacked. There was less dirt around. He poked his head into the bedroom.

Jordan was lying on his back, hands behind his head, asleep and breathing gently. It was stifling in the small bedroom. Sweat matted the hair on his chest and head. Ballantine lowered himself on the other bed.

"Brady!"

Jordan shook himself like a cat splashed with water. He rotated his neck gingerly as if it were stiff.

"It's been like a sauna bath all day. I couldn't get near the water. Those people were up and down the beach all day." His eyes asked the unvoiced question.

Ballantine looked at the glowing end of his cigarette. "Kyle killed her himself, Brady."

The other man's body coiled like a spring. "How do you know? What makes you say that?"

"They were in the garden," said Ballantine. "Kyle and the girl. He told her everything. I was standing behind the wall."

Jordan's fingers were drumming on the side of the bed. "Kyle. Then it *was* Kyle." He said it as if committing the fact to memory.

Ballantine explained. "He slipped out of the house. Neither his daughter nor the woman knew anything about it. They were saying what they thought was the truth. He followed Joanne here. It was his car that you heard, Brady. He must have been leaving as you arrived."

Jordan wiped his forehead with the back of his hand and looked at the sweat. "She never had a chance, Scott. That bastard never gave her a chance. You got the check?" He looked up quickly.

Ballantine nodded. "You're not going to like this, Brady. I'm taking it back."

Jordan's fingers stopped their drumming abruptly. He looked like a man who has just taken a bullet in the heart.

"You're going to do *what?*" he demanded.

Ballantine hesitated. "Joanne's dead. There's nothing you can do that will change things. I've seen something this afternoon that I'd sooner forget. I don't want that kind of money, Brady. Do what you like but the check goes back."

"You're putting me on," Jordan said belligerently. "What is it you *really* want?"

Ballantine sat for a moment, searching for an answer that would make sense. "I don't know," he said at last. "I'm sorry."

An ominous note in Jordan's voice underlined his tenseness. "You're sorry! I've got news for you, buster. I don't want that kind of money either. I want Kyle in the gas

189

chamber. And I've come too far to be loused up by a vaudeville Lancelot. I want that check."

Ballantine dropped his butt on the floor. He put his toe on it and ground out the glow. "George *was* right. You were always the one to watch. You've been using me from the beginning. But not anymore. I've opted out."

Both men were sitting perfectly still. The threat of impending violence hung between them like pepper in the air. There was something unnatural in the set of Jordan's face — the fixed stare that held Ballantine like a vise. He reached beneath his pillow swiftly. His eyes were the color of a cold mountain stream. It was the second time that day that a gun had been leveled at Ballantine.

"I'll kill you if I have to," Jordan warned. "I swear to God. Give me the check and get out of here."

Ballantine came up slowly. The sound of the breaking sea registered in his brain as if for the last time. He pushed his hand into his pocket and let the check flutter down. It fell on the bed in front of Jordan. The next moves were like a sequence from a speeded-up film. As Jordan reached for the check, the Canadian dove sideways, grabbing at Jordan's hand. He wrenched the gun from the other's grasp. His fingers found the trigger guard. A shell smacked into the wall behind them. His eyes and nose stung from the explosion, his ears were deafened. The two men rolled on the bed in a grunting wrestle. The gun fell to the floor. Ballantine jabbed hard with forked fingers, finding his opponent's eyeballs. Jordan's eyes streamed but he fought on with vicious cunning. His knee crashed against Ballantine's pelvic bone, missing its goal by inches. The Canadian locked both his hands and rammed the double fist at Jordan's throat. Jordan gasped, his head thudding back against the wall.

Ballantine twisted off the bed, kicking the gun out of reach. He snatched up the check from a fold in the crumpled blankets. "You're sick, man — *sick!*" It was all he could manage to say.

A snarling sound persisted through Jordan's strangled breathing. His bloodshot eyes sought Ballantine's face. "I'm going to kill you, Scott."

The Canadian bent swiftly, taking the other's launched body on the small of his back. He found the hand groping for his throat and pivoted sharply. He was behind Jordan now, the man's arm trapped in a half nelson. Jordan's mule kick landed on Ballantine's shin. It raked down the bone, drawing a gasp of pain. Ballantine brought Jordan's arm up slowly, steeling himself as he felt the shoulder blade dislocate. Jordan sank to his knees, right arm and shoulder drooping. He stayed like that for a second, like a man at prayer. Then he toppled sideways, hitting the boards with his head. He lay quite still, breathing stertorously.

Ballantine felt under the bed. The barrel of the gun was still warm from the explosion. He staggered down the porch steps toward the water. He threw the weapon as far as he could. It curved in an arc, flashing in the sunlight and sank without trace. A gull swooped in low over the deserted beach, planing away as it saw the solitary figure. Ballantine bent and splashed his face with the cool salt water. He walked back to the house. Jordan had not

191

moved. He was still lying with his injured shoulder beneath him. Ballantine lifted the phone. He dialed the number with infinite care. An eternity passed before he heard the ringing tone, another till he heard the woman's voice answer. It was sharp with anxiety.

"Daisy Palumbo — who is this calling?"

He pinned his elbow on the table, holding the receiver. Each word was an effort. "Scott Ballantine. You'd better get up here as fast as you can. And bring a doctor with you!"

His head drooped. Daisy Palumbo's voice came from a distance. "Come where — where are you speaking from — can you hear me, Scott?"

"Las Rosas — it's six, seven, miles out of Pacific Ramparts. You want Doc Carberry's house," he said woodenly. "Get Brady out of here while you can."

Her voice was coming and going. "What's *happened* to Brady?" He leaned his head on the table. Flies were crawling over the beer-stained map. He brushed them away as if it mattered. Mrs. Palumbo's voice rattled on. ". . . a whole day without letting me know what had happened to him. The sheriff's here, is a friend of mine. He knows the right people in Fairfax. You tell Brady that the Kyle house is being watched — do you understand?"

There was a manic reasoning in her voice that shocked him out of his lethargy. "Do what you're told. Brady hasn't been near the place."

Her presence projected itself into the room, bird bright and belligerent. "Then you see that he doesn't. *You're* the one who's responsible for all this. We know all about you

192

down here, Mr. Scott Ballantine. And if anything happens to Brady . . ."

He hung up the phone. His trouser bottoms were dripping water onto the floorboards. He got up stiffly and went down the steps. He broke into a shambling run as his feet touched the sand. He made Pacific Ramparts in eight minutes flat, jumped two sets of signals out of town, and pushed the accelerator down to the floor. He saw the Oak Valley marker coming up and wrenched the wheel over. Tires scattered the gravel on the driveway. He changed gear, regaining traction. He was cramming movement into the fewest seconds possible — as if time were running out. He roared out of the oak thicket and killed the motor. The rear end of the Rolls showed in the garage. He leaned on the steering wheel for a second. The garden was peaceful in the evening sunshine. The gum trees threw long shadows across the lawn. A strange hush hung over everything, as though the house were waiting for his return. The French windows leading into the study were open. He was glad that Kyle was back — glad not to have to face the girl again. He had no idea what he was going to say to the Englishman. Probably nothing. There was nothing to say. Just give the check back and leave. He wanted neither gratitude nor explanation, no further involvement. His own moral values were intact. He was neither judge nor defense counsel. He was going back where he'd started a couple of days ago: without money, without Jordan, but free.

He climbed out of the car. His stiffening muscles were a reminder of the savagery of his fight with Jordan. His shirt was ripped down the back, his shinbone agony where

193

Jordan's shoe had scored it. He walked around the pool toward the study. A sodden newspaper floated just beneath the surface of the water as if its reader had sprung up in haste.

He stopped in the open French windows, sniffing the odor of exploded cordite once again. Instinct told him to turn and run — to get out of this place as fast as he could. Something stronger than fear urged him forward. He stepped into the room, photographing the scene with his mind.

Kyle's body was lying on the floor over by the desk, arms and legs spread, head down. The Webley revolver Ballantine had seen that afternoon had skidded across the polished boards to the edge of the carpet. The girl was sitting on the couch, her knees huddled in her arms. She looked at him as a sleepwalker does, as though she had no sense of the past or the future. His first thought was for Kyle. He crossed the room and knelt, gathering the heavy body in his arms. The Englishman's eyes were shut. Blood wormed from his open mouth and his nostrils. More blood matted the white hair above his right ear. Tiny splinters of bone glistened in the burned purple hole there. Ballantine's reaction was involuntary. The dead man's head thudded back on the boards. Ballantine hauled himself up, wiping his sweating palms on his trousers. His voice cracked.

"Well for crissakes don't just sit there — *say* something!"

She looked as if she hadn't heard. He stumbled as he stepped toward her, bent down, and retrieved the gun he had trodden on. He put it on the desk and continued to the couch. He threw his hand out as if the gesture would unlock her tongue.

194

"Talk!" he urged. "Get a hold of yourself and talk!"

Time lengthened as they stared at one another. Then her eyes came to life. She spoke in a dull voice as a child might do, repeating a lesson that is too difficult.

"You killed him!"

It was a moment before he realized what she meant. He sat down beside her and pulled the check out.

"I came back to give you this, Tina."

She looked at him stonily. Suddenly his control snapped. He found himself shouting, waving the check in her face.

"*Look* at it, goddamn you!" He lit a match and held it to the slip of paper till the check curled in ashes. He ground them to a powder in his palm. "*I* killed your father — you're insane!"

She nodded as though agreeing. "Your finest hour."

He held himself in with an effort. She was dangerously near hysteria. Better she talked — no matter what she said.

"Listen to me," he said steadily. "There are things we have to do. First of all you've got to tell me what happened."

Her eyes considered him as if he had only recently arrived. "I told him that you had been here and taken the check away. I said we couldn't hope for mercy. He must have known then what he was going to do. He sent Mrs. Bruce into town. He wanted me to go too but I stayed." The fact seemed to be important to her. "I stayed. You drove an old man to suicide."

He lifted his hands hopelessly. Doubt niggled at his mind. Just how far had he driven Kyle to his death — how far was he excused by Jordan's treachery? He looked at her again, moved by her vulnerability.

195

"You'll have to call the police. Did your father leave any sort of a message — a letter, maybe?"

She was pulling at a thread in her skirt, her eyes averted. "I haven't looked. I couldn't go near him."

He opened all the drawers in the desk. The check stubs were still there. There was nothing that looked like a suicide note. He came back to her, wanting her to understand.

"You're on your own and you've got to face facts. There's no evidence against your father anymore — *nothing*. What you tell the police is your own business, but there's something you'd better remember. Involve me and you involve him. It's not a threat. I want you to see things clearly. The moment I've gone you're going to get on that line and yell for help. You don't have to lie. All you have to do is sit on part of the truth.

The hostility had gone from her face. Her voice was almost humble. "I'm alone in the house. At least stay with me till Mrs. Bruce comes back. You owe me that much."

He suddenly saw himself surrounded by a bunch of hard-nosed cops. Who was he and what was he doing there? He shook his head, aware of the mess his clothes were in.

"I owe you nothing. Make no mistake. I've come as far as I'm going."

She pulled herself up, passing her hand across her face. He saw the blood on the inside of her shirt sleeve. She'd lied when she told him that she hadn't been near Kyle's body. Suspicion flashed in his mind as he watched her. *She'd* shot her father! Fear and love had trapped her in some twilight world of her own. Sooner than see her father die in the gas chamber, she had killed him herself. That was why she wanted someone to stay — not to be alone. She

196

needed a voice — a hand — something she could reach for in the darkness.

The dog's bark sounded upstairs, sharp and anxious. Her eyes were watching every move that he made. He found himself remembering their look as they had faced one another earlier that afternoon, her father's gun against his chest. He was wrong. Neither fear nor love could make her kill. He was suddenly glad for himself and for her. He turned slowly and walked outside. The sodden newspaper had sunk lower in the pool. The shadows on the lawn were longer.

A flurry of startled birds winged through the air as he started the motor. He looked back at the house, relieved to be out of it. He'd done what he could for her. There were times when doing your best would never be enough. She'd go on living — adjust — the way everyone else did. It wasn't too hard to adjust if you had money and a roof over your head. All of them had something or someone, Jordan included. Aunt Daisy would be hurrying north by now. The hell with them. Nobody was going to worry about Ballantine. He let the car roll forward. He'd no intention of returning to Las Rosas. He had his identification papers with him, whatever was left of his money. The balance of Jordan's cash was back in the beach house. He stepped on the brakes at the road junction, hesitating whether to turn east or west. The Chevrolet was registered in his name. It would be no problem to sell in Los Angeles. Whatever it made would be little enough for his hire. What he'd *do* in L.A. was something else again. What the hell else had he ever done but play roles other people cast him in. He smiled suddenly. Maybe George

197

would have an idea. He wheeled the car west. Why not? It was what George had wanted all the time. He'd call the camp from Pacific Ramparts.

He'd gone a little more than five miles when he heard the police siren. The Highway Patrol car came around wide on the next bend, approaching from the opposite direction. Its lights flashed in the gathering dusk. For a moment he thought the car was going to pass. The next second put him right. The patrol car veered left and slewed in front of the Chevrolet. He stopped the motor and sat quite still, watching the two men walking toward him. They flanked the Chevrolet, moving without haste, guns drawn. He could see their faces now. They were identical in expression. They looked like wary cats stalking unknown territory. The cop on his side lifted his gun fractionally.

"Out, buddy!"

Ballantine obeyed. He held his arms high in the air. The cop used his free hand in a rapid search of Ballantine's clothing. He flipped the wallet open and read through the Canadian's identification. He called through the window to the other man. "Did you find anything?"

His partner tipped the seat forward and rummaged in the glove compartment. "Nothing. What do you think?"

The driver was chewing gum, his lower jaw moving like a cow's. He looked at Ballantine's clothing, slitting his eyes as he saw the lump on his cheekbone.

"Where you heading for, mister?"

"Pacific Ramparts."

"Where've you just come from?"

A light came on, pinpointing the house beyond the citrus

groves in front of them. Nothing had ever looked so far away.

"Oak Valley," Ballantine said slowly. "Can I put my hands down?"

The cop's breathing was heavy. "One at a time and real slow," he invited. He snapped a pair of handcuffs on Ballantine with the dexterity of a conjuror. The Canadian looked at his wrists, stupefied. "Now wait a minute . . ."

The cop cut him short. "Save it. I'm going to walk you back to the patrol car, mac. Let's not be ambitious, huh?"

They moved in on him, their shoulders sandwiching his body between them. The light was still flashing in front. One of the cops shoved Ballantine into the back of the patrol car and sat down heavily beside him. The driver leaned forward, speaking into the radiophone.

"Car seven-two calling in. Give me the Fairfax County Sheriff Department, Clive."

The dispatcher checked the message. Seconds later a deeper voice sounded in the box. There was a babble of noise in the background. "Fairfax County Sheriff Department. Sheriff Kowalsky speaking."

The driver's tone was impersonal. "State Highway Patrol, Sheriff. Officers Lopez and Mayer. It's on that A.P.B. of yours. Looks like we might have something for you. We picked a guy up five minutes ago, traveling west on Route 28. White, male, thirty-six, carrying identification in the name of Scott Ballantine. He's driving a black Chevrolet sedan, 1964 model. He claims he just left the Kyle place. What do you want us to do with him?"

Kowalsky's answer was prompt. "Take him back there.

You'll see the marker near the reservoir. I'm on my way."

The driver flipped up the call switch. He twisted in his seat to look at Ballantine. "You heard the man, buddy. You can do your talking there."

The patrol car surged forward. The suddenness of the acceleration slammed Ballantine back in his seat. What was happening to him seemed like a scene from some nightmare. There was the same combination of the sinister with a total lack of reason. A few minutes ago he'd been free. Now he was a cuffed prisoner being carried away at seventy miles an hour, lights flashing, siren wailing. The two cops were completely at ease, chatting to one another about some pile-up they had witnessed earlier. He might have been a stray dog they were taking to the pound.

He forced his brain to function. The driver had talked of an A.P.B. — an All Points Broadcast — apparently connected with the fact that he'd been at Oak Valley. But *why?* Aunt Daisy wouldn't have blown the whistle on him if only for Jordan's sake. There could only be one other person: Tina Kyle. And that made no sense either unless — and this was a point — he was technically a housebreaker. He'd gone in uninvited and removed a check for $375, the property of one ———. Now wait a minute, just whose property *was* the check anyway? She must be out of her mind.

The cop beside him stirred as Ballantine sat straighter. Maybe it *wasn't* for housebreaking. Suppose she'd blown the whole bit — her father's confession — everything. Then he and Jordan were extortionists. There was no time to explore the thought further. The driver was pulling off the

200

highway and up through the oak thicket. He cut the motor and cocked his head. The white fencing around the paddock glimmered in the twilight. The entire house was ablaze, as if someone had run from room to room flipping the light buttons. The big lamp was on above the pool, deepening the surrounding shadows. The station wagon had been left outside the garage. The housekeeper must have returned. The driver eased himself from his seat.

"Wait here, Al. I'll get the door."

He walked four yards and rapped with the butt of his gun looking up at the second-story windows. "Open up, Miss Kyle!" he called. "Police!" The bolts were drawn on the front door. A crack of light widened, tentatively and then generously. Tina Kyle and the housekeeper were standing in the hallway. Mrs. Bruce had an arm wrapped around the girl's shoulders. Her free hand was holding a meat cleaver. The driver took it away from her hastily. "OK, bring him in, Al!"

Tina Kyle backed off as Ballantine came through the doorway. The blood on her shirt sleeve had dried to a cake of dark brown. She put her hands up as if defending herself from a blow. Her eyes were wild and her mouth round with fear.

"Don't let him come near me! No! *Please!*"

It was convincing and the driver put himself between her and Ballantine. He motioned to the housekeeper. Mrs. Bruce moved to the girl's side again.

"Everyone take it easy," the cop said.

Headlights swept through the oak thicket. A car door banged outside. Sheriff Kowalsky lumbered into the hallway like a bear disturbed at the honey pot. He nodded at the patrolman, touched the brim of his hat for Tina Kyle, and looked at Ballantine last of all.

"I got a deputy outside," he warned, "hasn't fired a gun in months. He'll be real anxious. Understand?"

Ballantine nodded. He tried to wet his lips but found no spittle. "I want to explain . . ." he began.

Kowalsky ignored him. He removed his Stetson, wiped the top of his head, and put his hat on again. "Where's your father, Miss Kyle?"

She led the way along the corridor, dry eyed and erect. Once in the study, the patrolman released Ballantine's sleeve, shut the door behind them, and put his back against it. The Canadian's cuffs rattled as he tried to catch Kowalsky's attention. Kyle's body was lying in the same position but the gun was no longer on the desk. It was on the carpet near the French windows. He turned his head sharply and caught the girl watching him. He read the truth in her eyes as plainly as if she had spoken. Neither fear nor love could put the will to kill in her. But hatred could. He suddenly knew what was coming.

His fingerprints were on that gun. She'd have seen enough television to know how to move the weapon from the desk to the floor without touching the revolver herself. Kowalsky rose from the dead man's side.

"You men gone over him?" he asked.

"He's clean, Sheriff," the driver answered laconically. "There was nothing in his car."

Kowalsky loomed over the Canadian. He pushed his face near enough for Ballantine to smell peppermint over beer. "Siddown on that couch and keep your goddamn mouth shut. I'll tell you when to talk."

The dog was barking frantically. The patrolman let the housekeeper through the door. The barking subsided. Kowalsky picked up the phone and dialed.

"Hank? This is Sheriff Kowalsky. Get hold of Doc Rahvis. Tell him to come on out to the Kyle place. And send an ambulance. Sure he's dead! What do you think this is, Hank, a goddamn ball game? You want a play by play! Get hold of Rahvis."

He lowered his buttocks onto the edge of the desk. He coughed gently, looking at the girl.

"You wanna tell us what happened, Miss Kyle? Take your time and don't worry about a thing."

He spoke as though the occasion were provided for his benefit. Tina Kyle was standing as far away from Ballantine as she could, beyond the desk and in front of a bookcase. She looked at the sheriff, her fingers working nervously, and took a deep breath.

"It must have been some time after five. My father was down here alone. He was going over this script and didn't want to be disturbed. I was upstairs in my room. My father had sent Mrs. Bruce into town for something. I noticed that the dog kept going to the door and whining. After a while I went to the top of the stairs. I could hear men's voices in the study — loud, as if they were arguing. Then I heard my father shout 'No!'" She covered her face with her hands. The room waited till she pulled herself together again.

"I must have been halfway down the stairs when I heard

a shot. I opened the study door and saw my father lying where he is now. That man was standing near the desk. I might have said something. I can't remember. But I know I was too scared to move. He was pointing the gun at me. Suddenly he turned and ran. He dropped the gun as he went through the windows."

"She's lying!" The patrolman shoved Ballantine back in his seat. The Canadian shook his hand off. "She's lying!" he said again. "I was here but it wasn't like that — none of it!"

Kowalsky shifted on the desk. "You ever see this guy before, Miss Kyle?"

She looked Ballantine full in the face. It was a frank and appraising look as though even now she would give him the benefit of the doubt. She shook her head decisively. "Never!"

"How about the gun, Miss Kyle?" It was the patrolman standing behind Ballantine.

She nodded quickly. "It was my father's. He's had it as long as I can remember. This is a lonely house. We sometimes keep money in the safe."

Kowalsky picked at a hair in his ear. "Don't worry about the gun. We issued the permit." He came across and stood over Ballantine again. "OK, feller. I've got a hunch that you know all the ropes. You don't have to say a damn thing to me but whatever you do say is gonna stay right here!" He tapped his right temple meaningly.

Ballantine's escort shifted a couple of yards, leaving the floor to the sheriff. The Canadian's head drooped.

"I'll talk but you've got to listen," he muttered. "Kyle

204

was where he is now when I came through those windows. And she was right here, sitting on the couch, alone with him. The only time I touched him was to turn him over. He was already dead."

Kowalsky's palm cupped Ballantine's chin, forcing it up. "What were you doing here, anyway?"

Four people hung on his answer. "Bringing something back to her. A check drawn by Kyle for $375."

Kowalsky stepped back as if he had trodden on a live wire. "A check, huh? And where is it now?"

Ballantine moved his head defeatedly. "*She* knows where it is. I put a match to it in front of her."

Kowalsky started a slow and understanding smile. His wink for the patrolmen took the edge off it. "Now how about that, he *burned* it!" His manner changed abruptly. "You know a guy called Brady Jordan?"

"I know him." Even to his own ears the admission sounded guilty.

Kowalsky glanced at the officers and spread his legs wide. "You bet you know him! He sent you here, didn't he? There never *was* any goddamn check. You bums thought you could stampede an old man into parting with money. But Kyle had too much guts. How'd you get those torn clothes — who marked you up? I'll tell you who, son. Kyle pulled that gun to protect himself. You took it away from him and put a bullet in his brain."

"No," said Ballantine. He looked from one to the other and found no hope. "Can't you see that I'm telling the truth?" he asked desperately.

Kowalsky's eyes were cunning. "Maybe you wiped the

gun off. But the wax'll tell whether you fired it or not."

Ballantine shook his head dumbly, remembering. They dipped your hand in a coating of paraffin wax or something and the test was infallible. He *had* fired a gun — Jordan's. He wanted to scream the words at them, again and again till they believed him. He imagined what a prosecutor would say. The evidence of the girl. The defendant's fingerprints on the weapon. The undeniable proof that he had fired a gun. And a motive.

He barely opened his eyes, seeing the room like a stage set: the body on the floor, the circle of hostile faces, the one prop that had somehow not been moved. The revolver was stilly lying on the floor near the windows. *Act,* he thought on impulse, *and for once in your life be convincing!*

He came off the sofa, his mouth working. "All right!" he yelled, then he started to laugh. His whole body was shaking. The three men were surprised into momentary inertia. Ballantine wheeled and fell on the gun. He came up holding the heavy weapon in his manacled hands. Kneeling, he leveled the barrel at the girl.

"Nobody move!" he warned. He scrambled up to his feet.

The patrolman by the door unfroze a little. Kowalsky's instruction came sharply. "Do as he says!"

Ballantine's thumb cocked the heavy trigger. "The truth," he ordered hoarsely. "Tell them the truth!"

Tina Kyle crossed her arms on her chest. Her voice was very quiet. "You killed my father!"

He felt the sweat trickling down his ribs. He read her final triumph. The others would see no more than a girl with courage. The looks on their faces had hardened to open condemnation. Nothing to do now but run. He retreated slowly to the windows, switching his aim to the sheriff. The French windows were locked. He dare not turn to unfasten them. He backed through the panes of glass bodily. The broken fragments crashed outside. Slivers cascaded into his hair and clothing. He swiveled and ran, skidding on the damp tiles. The gun went in his flight. He heard it hit the ground.

It was as bright as day in this part of the garden. The men in the study had started to shout. A shot shattered the evening, the bullet whining away to his left. A sideways glance found the deputy kneeling by the parked cars. He was taking fresh aim. Ballantine ran like a hunted hare, zigzagging toward the darkness at the back of the stables. The shouting behind was louder, as if the officers were in the garden now. He threw himself through the post-and-rail fencing. Splinters of glass sliced into his flesh. He ran blindly, with no sense of direction, gulping air into his overworked lungs. Muscles faltered. He broke into a shambling trot that ended in a headlong fall among the ferns. His legs were as useless as his hands. Somehow he had to rid himself of the handcuffs. He thought of the Chevrolet somewhere out there, parked on the highway. There were tools in it. Even if he could find the car, there'd be a stake-out. He rolled over on his back, staring up at the sky. Stars blinked through the curtain of night. The shouting had stopped — or maybe he'd run himself out of earshot. They were probably waiting for reinforcements. He picked himself up again, willing himself to continue. No chance trying to hitch a ride wearing a pair of police manacles. He was dead unless he could rid himself of them. He slowed again, to a walk now, trying to conserve his breathing. The crescent of the rising moon gave him a sense of orientation. He was a mile away from the house and heading east, parallel with Route 28. After a while he came to trees. He accepted their cover gratefully. Small eyes stared at him from the darkness. Unseen things scuttled from him in the darkness. Suddenly he stopped. It was no good. He should never have run in the first place. Innocent men never run. He let himself down to the ground and propped his back against a tree trunk. It was difficult to drag the battered pack of cigarettes from his pocket. There was one left. He smoked it with a sense of finality. There *was* no place to go. All he could do was sit here and wait for them. The pink streaks of false dawn were showing when he heard the hounds baying in the distance. The sound grew nearer, chilling and ominous. He'd crossed no water, his scent would be strong. Then two searchlights pierced the trees, way over his head. They must be using jeeps. Cars could never have followed his trail. The beams crisscrossed, scissors of light searching the wood at ground level now. The hounds were close — maybe fifty yards away. He could hear the shouts of the handlers.

He scrambled up and ran after the light. He wanted nothing more than to be found — to talk to someone who would listen. He held his handcuffed wrists high in front of him and yelled as loudly as he could.

"Here! Over on the left! *Here!*"

A searchlight found him, pinning him like a moth. It blinded him completely. He could hear people running through the trees. He shielded his eyes with his arms. A ring of hostile faces surrounded him. One man was holding back a brace of straining hounds. Kowalsky stepped out of the throng. His hat was gone, his breeches snagged and stained. The whining of the hounds was the only sound in the sudden silence. The sheriff doubled his fist and measured his man. The powerful blow sank deep into Ballantine's solar plexus.

The next thing he knew he was sitting on a chair. His chest was covered with dried vomit. Someone had taken off the handcuffs. He concentrated on the sign on the glass-topped door till it made sense.

FAIRFAX COUNTY
SHERIFF DEPARTMENT

Kowalsky and a deputy were sitting across the room watching him. The clock above their heads read twenty past six. There was a strong smell of whisky. Kowalsky had changed his breeches. His hat was still missing. He lowered his legs from an upturned trash basket.

"That was a damfool thing to do! Put me to a whole heap of trouble, you know that?" He sounded like some kindly teacher, reproving childish behavior.

Ballantine's gasp was involuntary. Pain probed at his body in a dozen places. Worst of all was the bruising ache in the pit of his stomach. He managed to speak out unsteadily.

"You're making the biggest mistake you ever made."

209

Two faces grinned at him. Kowalsky shook his head in mock wonder. "Hear that, Hank? Now there's something you oughta be thinking about, Hank. You know the county don't like mistakes."

The deputy snickered dutifully. Daylight streamed through the windows. The flat-topped desk had a rail on three sides, fencing in the wads of paper. Kowalsky's gun rested on a book. Ballantine read the title: *Gardening for Beginners.* Kowalsky yawned.

"See if you can get some coffee, Hank. It's been a long night and Scott here wants to sit and talk awhile."

The deputy undid the door. He locked it again from the outside. Kowalsky stretched out, bringing the gun a little closer. He looked at Ballantine meditatively.

"I got a make on you, Scott. Five-to-six for burglary. They let you out of Springfield just three days ago. Whose idea was this — yours or Brady's?"

Ballantine shook his head. Kowalsky would talk before he would listen. The sheriff picked at a loose filling.

"Ain't gonna do you no good," he observed mildly. "Your partner's over in the County Hospital, hollowin' his head off. He claims it was your idea to shake down Kyle. He says you told him that you'd worked with Kyle — that you had something on him. Says you conned him into parting with eighteen hundred dollars expense money."

Ballantine stared back contemptuously. It was the oldest caper in the game. And if it wasn't a caper, it still didn't matter.

"Lies."

Kowalsky shook his head regretfully. "Miz Palumbo's

not lying, Scott. She caught on to you before Brady did. Jordan wanted out at the last moment. So you broke his collarbone."

Words and facts no longer seemed to mean anything. Guilt became innocence and innocence guilt. And the beginning of it all seemed to have been forgotten. He recalled it now, deliberately.

"You don't believe in the check. Suppose I told you that it was Kyle who killed his wife? That I heard him tell his daughter?"

Kowalsky's grin widened. "I'd call you a goddamn liar, son. It don't even hold together. The other does."

Ballantine's voice was bitter. "You don't *want* it to hold together do you, Sheriff? It exposes you for what you are, a blundering butcher. There *was* a check and I found it. I was out at Oak Valley twice yesterday — the last time to take the check back. There's a bar in Pacific Ramparts — the guy'll remember. I fought with Jordan long before Kyle's death. Check the time of the call I made to Mrs. Palumbo."

Kowalsky creaked forward, his manner insinuating. "But you did go back and gun that man, Scott. I'm trying to help you, son. If Jordan's lying, if he's in this all the way with you, ain't no reason in the wide world why you gotta take this rap on your own. Understand what I mean?"

Ballantine's answer was shaky. "You bet I understand." They measured one another silently. Each had gone as far as he would and both knew it. Kowalsky pulled a bunch of keys from a drawer.

"OK, feller. Let's move it. You'll get your coffee in the county jail."

211

Ballantine stood. Even to shrug was agony. "Don't I have the right to call a lawyer?"

The sheriff pulled the phone over. "Sure do, son. One call — to a friend, relative, or legal adviser. What's his number?"

Ballantine licked his lips. The salivary glands were working now. "You'll find it in the book. The name's Donatelli."

>>> If you've enjoyed this book and would like to discover more great vintage crime and thriller titles, as well as the most exciting crime and thriller authors writing today, visit: >>>

The Murder Room
Where Criminal Minds Meet

themurderroom.com